STORIES OF US

Bobby Sachdeva is a storyteller by choice and a businessman by profession. He writes stories to highlight the problems with norms and standards in our changing society. In all the stories, Bobby Sachdeva engages with the problems in the lives of common people and the ways to resolve these. Filmmakers have shown interest and some of these short stories are being adapted for short films now. Bobby Sachdeva lives in Amritsar with his family and owns a film studio, Ajab Productions. This is his first book.

STORIES OF US

The Common Man

Changing Perceptions

Bobby Sachdeva

PAN

First published 2019 by Pan
an imprint of Pan Macmillan Publishing India Private Limited,
707, Kailash Building
26 K. G. Marg, New Delhi – 110 001
www.panmacmillan.co.in

Pan Macmillan, 6 Briset St, Farringdon, London EC1M 5NR
Basingstoke and Oxford
Associated companies throughout the world
www.panmacmillan.com

ISBN 978-93-89109-02-3

This is a work of fiction. All characters, locations and events are fictitious. Any resemblance to actual events or locales or persons, living or dead, is entirely coincidental.

1 3 5 7 9 8 6 4 2

Typeset in Scala by Manmohan Kumar
Printed and bound in India by
Replika Press Pvt. Ltd.

CONTENTS

BOARDED
RESERVE BANK OF INDIA
₹500
0AB 123456
APPROVED

1

BOARDING PASS

Mr Verma is a fifty-year-old, well-educated, good-looking yet humble person. He is standing at the Shanghai Airport, queued up for the business-class passengers at the check-in counter. He is dead tired after a hectic work day in China and is listening to music on headphones to relax. So tired is he that he does not realize he is standing in the business-class section with an economy-class ticket!

Just then, an Indian-Punjabi businessman, Mr Rajan Mehta, in his late forties, comes and stands behind Mr Verma. There were another four men ahead of him in the queue. Mr Verma's phone beeps with an incoming email. He turns off the music, takes off the headphones, and checks his email. Mr Mehta, impressed with Mr Verma's personality, initiates a conversation by introducing himself as a builder based in Delhi catering to the corporate sector and making big commercial buildings. His business had brought him to China to study the latest developments in office designing.

Mr Verma introduces himself as an engineer from IIT Kanpur visiting China to inspect new machines for his factory in Delhi. Mr Mehta continuously tells him about his current and future projects to make an impression of how big his business is.

When Mr Verma proceeds to the check-in counter, the woman informs him that he is in the wrong queue and directs him towards the economy-class section. Mr Verma realizes his mistake, but because he is extremely tired requests her to issue his boarding pass. The woman seems a little irritated, but seeing just one other passenger behind him, issues his boarding pass. Next is Mr Mehta. He keeps his boarding pass in his pocket in a manner that 'Business Class' is clearly visible. Both passengers now proceed towards the boarding gate and find that their flight is delayed by an hour. Mr Mehta invites Mr Verma for dinner at the airport's best eating place – a seafood restaurant that serves French wine and caviar. Mr Mehta orders caviar and wine; Mr Verma settle for simple fish and chips and local Chinese beer. After dinner, Mr Mehta insists on paying the bill. They now indulge in informal talks about their families. Mr Verma talks about his twenty-five-year-old son who works with him in his factory. He shows his photograph – a tall, handsome boy standing in front of the gate of a big building, which Mr Mehta assumes to be his factory.

Mr Mehta tells Mr Verma that he has been looking for a suitable 'high-class' match for his beautiful twenty-three-year-old daughter and expresses interest in forging a new relationship between the two. He would like to meet his son and introduce him to his daughter giving them time to interact before the families can proceed with formalities. Their conversation is still on when they hear the boarding announcement for their flight. They proceed towards the boarding gate talking about the possibilities of a match. They even exchange their phone numbers.

On reaching the boarding gate, Mr Mehta gives way to Mr Verma to board. Suddenly, Mr Mehta notices 'Economy Class' on his boarding pass. He is shocked! Mr Verma is not a high-class man after all! His facial expressions change and he starts to feel uneasy.

Sensing his discomfort, Mr Verma tells him that he stood in the business-class queue by mistake, that he does belong to the cattle class, and that he is sorry for wasting his valuable time. He pauses and then continues: '*Aur haan, mujhe Business-class traveller samajhne ke saath saath shayad tumne mere bete ke peechhe wale sheds ko meri factory samajh li hogi. Meri to chhoti si factory hai. Yeh to Tata Engineers ka plant hai jahan mera beta teen din ki training pe gaya tha taaki apni factory ke liye kuchh nayi technology seekh sake.*' (Perhaps along with thinking I am a Business-class traveller you would have considered the sheds behind my son in the photograph to be my factory. I have a small factory. The one in the photograph is the Tata Engineers plant where my son attended a training session to learn about a new technology.)

Mr Mehta is numb with disbelief.

Mr Verma bids Mr Mehta farewell and proceeds towards his side of the boarding gate.

Question

Have we become so class-conscious that we judge people only by their appearance?

2

TRUE LOVE AND SUSPICION

Neha, in her mid-thirties, teaches psychology in a prestigious college in Mumbai. She had big dreams of an exciting life after marriage. Her husband, Dr Jayesh, on the other hand, is a serious and busy man. He is a dedicated gynaecologist with a good reputation and practices in a renowned hospital in the same city.

The couple loved each other and adjusted to each other's requirements. Neha wanted a child soon after getting married, but her husband was particular about her studies and career. After completing her studies, Neha did not start working because she did not want to raise a child under work pressure. But her husband disagreed.

Despite such a close bond, today Neha is standing outside the court holding divorce papers. She has divorced Jayesh.

It all begins when Neha catches Jayesh coming out of a hotel with a woman. When confronted, Jayesh accepts that she is a sex worker, but assures Neha that there was no physical contact. Neha becomes suspicious, when he refuses to reveal her identity, that her husband has cheated on her. Completely helpless, Jayesh accepts Neha's decision of a divorce. Even in court when he protects the woman's dignity, saying he does not want to tarnish her image, everyone is convinced of the charges against him. Overnight he loses his reputation and respect, and is fired from his job at the hospital.

With a shattered reputation, Jayesh moves to Nashik, whereas Neha joins a college to teach psychology. She becomes devoid of any emotion and crawls into a shell, away from the outer world. The only contact, albeit limited, she keeps is with her childhood friend, Shama.

She is engrossed in teaching and is happy with her batch of intelligent students. One of her students, Sameer, equally brilliant as the others, asks her a question one day: 'Why do husbands cheat?' Neha is shocked and replies bluntly, 'Because they are bastards.' The students look at each other in disbelief. They are merely asking from the point of male psyche, but Neha's frustration finds a vent and she makes one shocking statement after the other. She storms out of the class and goes straight to the dean's office to complain that the students ask unreasonable questions and that she cannot continue teaching the class. But the dean disagrees, saying it is the brightest lot, capable of seeking admission in renowned universities abroad. He asks her to review her decision and find the real reason of worry.

Neha calms down after stepping out of his office and realizes how deeply disturbed she is. She is in need of a break and decides to go to her hometown of Bengaluru to her friend Shama.

Neha asks her the same question her students asked her, to which Shama mockingly replies that in their community husbands are allowed four marriages, legally.

She returns to Mumbai to seek answers. She is out to find the woman who was with her husband on known streets, pick-up points, night clubs, and through brokers, but to no use. Sameer, her student, helps in her mission to locate this woman. They look through a popular website where these women are listed. After rigorous search, Neha stumbles upon a face that looks vaguely familiar. 'Interested in mature, sincere, and gentlemen ONLY', read her profile description – just the right match for Jayesh.

Sameer and Neha decide to book an appointment with her the following evening, stating Sameer as the potential client. But when they meet the woman Anupama, Sameer says that someone else would like to meet with her. The woman smiles and agrees to meet with Neha. Neha tells her that she only wants to talk about her profession because she is writing her thesis on the oldest profession in the world. Anupama, agrees to answer Neha's questions, but asks the kid in the room, Sameer, to leave. Feeling insulted, he leaves at once.

Anupama begins her story.

Her husband is an IT engineer based in the USA on work permit, but is not getting his permanent visa. It has been three years now and she has been loyal to him all this while. To satiate her physical needs, a friend of hers had suggested joining this trade like herself, whose husband too is away for the last five years.

After asking some more questions, Neha finally arrives at her main question, if she remembers her husband and the purpose of his visit. With some difficulty she remembers Jayesh and it seems she has a lot of respect for him. She tells Neha he had visited her on three occasions and asked her why women cheat, a question that had tormented him throughout his growing years. Jayesh's father had caught his mother cheating on him, but he decided to continue the marriage for the sake of their children. Jayesh remembered his parents sharing a disturbed relationship, and he hated both his parents, especially his mother, after learning the truth. Anupama also tells Neha that Jayesh felt relieved after talking to her and had expressed that he did not want to share this reality with his wife to maintain the dignity of his parents in front of her.

Anupama continues that she feels women get away with cheating because the men have to uphold their honour as it is a stab at their manhood. Because women have to don multiple hats at the same time, they are emotionally more stronger than men.

Neha now understands that Jayesh was right all along, that he did not cheat on her. She immediately decides to go to Nasik to Jayesh's clinic. She apologies to him and requests him to forgive her and accept her as his wife once again. Jayesh agrees without any hesitation.

Questions

Do we become suspicious about our partners or friends before carefully understanding the circumstances?

Is hasty decision-making in our fast-paced daily life leading to breakdown in relationships?

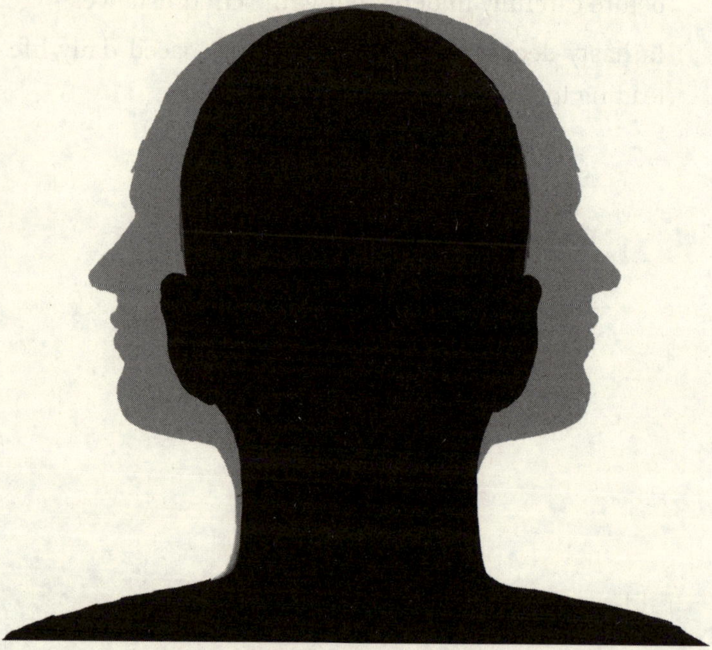

3
THE THIRD GENDER

This is an intense story of a sensitive issue of our society: an emotional journey of two eunuchs born into an educated middle-class family, separated and brought up differently because of fateful circumstances, and reunited thirty years later.

Disha and Arnav are a well-educated and open-minded couple residing happily in Meerut. Arnav holds a prestigious job in a private bank, while Disha is a teacher in a school. Within a year of their marriage, Disha conceives, and the couple is very happy to become parents. The day comes when Disha gives birth to a baby, but the long-awaited happiness is snatched away within moments when the doctor declares that the baby to be a eunuch. They are sad, but soon embrace the reality. Their main worry is how to keep the child with themselves as the whole hospital now knows that a eunuch is born. It is a stigma for such a child to be born. If news leaks from the hospital and the eunuch gang is informed in exchange of money, ultimately, the baby will be taken away by them from its parents to be raised in their community.

Fearing this, both Disha and Arnav plead with their doctor to protect their newborn, which the doctor agrees, but a ward boy, who works on a commission for the eunuch community, informs them. After Disha is discharged, the gang leader reaches their house to take away the child. There is a scuffle and the whole neighbourhood learns the truth about Disha and Arnav's baby. Despite reluctance, the child is taken away forcibly, leaving the new parents shattered.

Disha and Arnav are very supportive towards each other and try to adjust to the circumstances. They even approach the gang and plead them to return their baby several times, but looking at the manner they bring up children and the surroundings, they give up hope. Although time heals them, the void remains.

Disha and Arnav are expecting their second child making them happy once again, but with a tinge of fear. What if history repeats itself? To be absolutely sure, they consult a gynaecologist, Dr Sita, in Mumbai and urge her to reveal the sex of their unborn child. Since determination of sex of an unborn child is illegal, the doctor agrees to be silent in exchange for a huge sum of money. Unfortunately, this baby too is a hermaphrodite. They decide not to terminate the pregnancy and shift immediately to the suburbs of Mumbai to begin a new life.

Here, Arnav starts a small business of antiques, artefacts, and handicrafts, while Disha stays at home so that she can hide her pregnancy from neighbours. When it is time for the delivery, Dr Sita acts as the midwife against a large sum once again. They name the baby Ayesha and decide to bring her up in isolation and home tutor her, to keep her safe and with her parents. They tell the neighbours that their child is sick and hence has to stay at home.

Ayesha brings along good luck for her parents: Arnav's business flourishes. She enjoys luxuries and basks in the love of her parents, but is restrained from playing and interacting with other children.

On the other hand, Reeta, Disha and Arnav's first child, as named by the enuch gang, is being brought up under miserable conditions. At five she is forced to learn dance and is taught etiquettes of the hijra community. She is made to collect money at other hijras' performances, and although embarrassed and humiliated, she has to do her job.

But luck favours her in the form of her kind dance teacher, Bhushan, who treats her like his daughter. He recognizes her talent for dance and teaches her the classical form, and also takes time out to teach her to read and write Hindi. Reeta is a sharp child and picks up both with ease.

Around ten, Ayesha begins to notice some differences in her body compared to other women, like her mother and the maids. She becomes inquisitive and starts questioning. At first Disha tries to change the topic, but her questions continue growing more and more frequent. One day, finally, Disha and Arnav reveal the reality. She is taken aback and shattered. She is unable to forgive her parents for doing injustice to her by keeping her identity a secret. When she is still not convinced, they take her to the colony of eunuchs to show the real state of affairs and why she was being closeted. Ayesha understands and is thankful to her parents for the life they have given her.

Having learnt the truth, Ayesha now wants to see and experience the outside world. She wants to attend a real school. After much hesitation, her parents agree. She puts in a lot of hard work and does well. Her teachers appreciate her as well. She begins to lead the life of a regular person and even attracts male attention. While in college, the head of a notorious college gang approaches her, but she politely refuses. But the boy cannot take rejection and kidnap her along with his gang members and try to sexually assault her. She somehow gathers courage to fight back and escapes, but the incident leaves her shaken and scared to face the consequences if her identity is revealed.

Life continues much the same for Reeta. When she turns ten, she begins dancing at events. Her good looks and great dancing skills make her a star child among the hijras. The leader of the gang notices the luring eyes of people towards her. At fourteen, she is forced into the sex trade. Her clients are young and old drunk men who exploit her body. As a result, she suffers great mental and physical agony. But Reeta is strong from within and vents her frustration through dancing. She starts writing and singing her own songs and soon starts performing like professional choreographers. With age, Reeta stops selling her body. She now supervises junior hijras and teaches them dance. She continues to dance and write with the same enthusiasm.

Both Reeta and Ayesha are coping with life. Ayesha's hard work and determination proves fruitful and she becomes a successful entrepreneur at thirty. She will soon be awarded the 'Woman Entrepreneur of the Year' award. Many young, influential men express the desire to marry her, but she maintains safe distance, except Ashish, the CEO of an MNC.

Dr Sita is still in touch with Disha and Arnav, but for a reason. Since Ayesha's birth, she has been blackmailing them. Now that her daughter is going to be married, she demands more money, but Arnav is tired of her taunts and refuses to pay anymore. Angered by Arnav's refusal, Dr Sita rocks Ayesha's world once again by telling her about her sibling.

Memories of the past are refreshed. Wounds are reopened.

After learning the truth, Ayesha is determined to get Reeta home at any cost and takes Ashish's help. With his connections, Ashish is able to bribe the leader and free Reeta.

Disha and Arnav are overwhelmed to see their first child back home, but Reeta is angry and wants to know why she was abandoned. Slowly, they relive the painful past and make Reeta understand they had no choice. After much explanation, Reeta accepts their apologies and the family is reunited.

Ayesha realizes Reeta's potential as a dancer and writer. She helps with her grooming and opens an institute for her where she can teach dance. Finally, she gets the respect and fame of a dance teacher, something she has been yearning all this while.

The day arrives when Ayesha is going to be awarded for her hard work. When she goes up to accept the award, she realizes she cannot accept it under a false identity. This makes her refuse it and disclose her true gender – the third gender – to the audience. She explains hiding her real identity and living with phobia is not living a true life. It is the intelligence, dedication, and hard work that should matter, not the gender of the person, to be successful and live with dignity. She stands up for the third gender and encourages their education and support to live life like any other human being. Being born with a different body is no one's fault, and they should not be criminalized or ostracized.

There is silence. But the audience soon breaks into thunderous applause.

It is auspicious for eunuchs to perform and give blessings on festivals and during occasions of birth and wedding, and they are duly rewarded for this gesture. It is believed that their blessings are powerful and bring about good results. Money has lured many others; young boys from poor backgrounds either pretend to be eunuchs or surgically transform their bodies to be part of this lucrative trade. There are clashes between the eunuch community and those who pose to be them, and they mark their territories of profit. Since they cannot earn themselves any other respectable jobs, they are forced to resort to other means such as selling their bodies and beg. On a daily basis, today eunuchs face abuse and many hardships to earn their living.

Questions

Is our society being just in thinking and acting towards eunuchs as a separate community? Should the eunuchs get more support from the wider society for getting integrated in diverse professions to come out of their community and traditional practices?

4
LOVE IN THE TIMES OF WAR

Love and time share a bittersweet relationship; they have an unusual way of changing how and what we think of other people. The equations of human relationships constantly change over time and in turn change the course of the lives of those involved.

Alok and Bishan are business partners who have a lot of things in common. They are of the same age and their kids, Ayesha (Bishan's daughter) and Rishi (Alok's son) are childhood-friends-turned-lovers. Their life seems nothing short of perfect. But the reality is something else. Alok is a kind-hearted person and a philanthropist. He trusts Bishan and has given him his share of the work because he wants to devote his time to social work. However, Bishan is his friend's opposite: money-minded, cunning, selfish, and has his eyes on Alok's money.

Even with Alok's business in his hands, Bishan is greedy for more. He shifts funds and stocks from his friends's factory where he holds only a ten per cent share. But with this shift, the labour lose their salaries, materials lose their quality, and clients do not get timely deliveries. The labour goes on strike and Alok gets arrested for financial frauds, actually done by Bishan, and it takes no time for the company to go broke. Rishi, the next in line, also faces arrest, but he is in London. He decides to stay there, and in the meantime take this as an opportunity to unearth Bishan's wrongdoings. To make ends meet, he works in London as a waiter.

But the cunning man that Bishan is, he proves in court that Alok had transferred his ten per cent shares to his son and cheated him. All this while Bishan had been falsely taking Alok's signatures on the transfer papers, and Alok never cared to read them because he trusted his friend.

A similar story runs in the parallel, with Rishi and Ayesha and their college friends Smriti and Aryan. The four share a strong, inseparable bond. Because of her humble background, Aryan's extremely rich family harshly rejects Smriti. Aryan and Ayesha share the pain of broken hearts, while their families are set on a mission to dismiss their poor lovers. The strength and comfort of friendship overcomes the insecurity of love. The four friends hatch a plan. To satisfy their families' wishes and gain their confidence they decide that, Aryan and Ayesha, and Rishi and Smriti, will get married, work to unearth the secrets of fraud done by Bishan and once everything settles down, they will break their respective marriages and go back to their partners.

One day, Ayesha overhears her father Bishan confessing his crime. She becomes stronger in her resolve to fight for her love and justice. Rishi and Ayesha start collecting evidence and are joined by Bishan's secretary who has always been loyal to her first employer. Ayesha begins recording her father's conversations on his phone and transfers them to her phone while he is asleep.

Amidst all this, while he has amassed all possible wealth, Bishan is reduced to a lifeless statue, with a daughter who hates him and without Alok, a loyal friend he has betrayed – Bishan suffers a brain stroke and is left paralysed. Realization strikes him at this stage and he wants to confess and make everything right. He revives the two companies, his and Alok's, by infusing funds and inventories that he had stolen, and soon after that he dies. Alok is finally free now and Rishi returns home.

The children, who had planned the alliances with much zeal now feel it is not a game anymore. They certainly have won, but in the process people have died and new relationships have been forged. Circumstances have led to deep affection in the respective marriages.

For the divorce proceedings to be quicker, their lawyer suggests to file for divorce under infidelity. The former lovers decide to meet to talk things out. Aryan and Smriti share a mutual feeling of awkwardness and guilt, whereas Rishi and Ayesha force themselves to believe that they are still in love and make love, but they too finally realize there is nothing left between them. They leave heartbroken.

The lawyer hires two detectives to record the duration of the meetings to supply as proof in court. But the detective assigned for Rishi and Ayesha's meeting is cunning and records everything that happens in the room. He is aware of their family history and blackmails them to pay five crores, failing which he will leak the video. Hassled, they visit their lawyer for help.

The lawyer is experienced and wise, and is thus able to understand that neither couples want to go through divorce. He counsels them to accept the truth of the matter before handling the detective himself.

As for the real solution, he starts tracking the life and movements of his bad counterpart, and soon finds out that he cheats on his wife every night, on the pretext of going to work. He records this for proof and plays on the master – this detective, his own trick. He gives him a ransom call for 10 crores with the other option of switching the tapes. The detective who was trying to be the boss here, surrenders and ends this.

The divorce proceedings strengthen the bond of the new couples and they are finally out of denial of their feelings towards each other. They stand up for each other together and agree that they do not want the divorce.

The case is dismissed. They accept each other without any inhibition and with an open heart.

Questions

Are we aware of the change in our relationships with others constantly?

Do we accept when the unexpected happens in our lives and relationships?

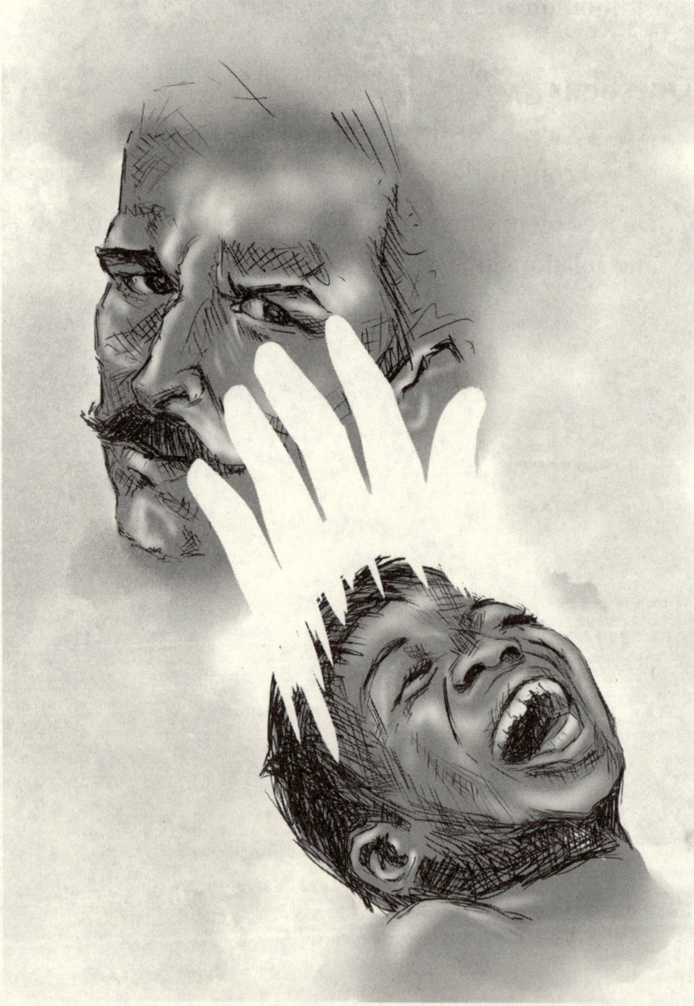

5
THE BRIGHT OLD SCOOTER

Desires and dreams do not always lead to good things. They are talked about as things that make us soar high, but sometimes they also make us shallow and vile. This is the story of Armaan, a young boy with big dreams but meagre means. His life has given him all the things that matter, the things that money cannot buy, in spite of this he has his eyes set on things that money can buy.

Armaan's father is a humble, honest, and righteous man. Even though he barely manages to make ends meet, he has never accepted bribes or adopted unfair means. He works a low-value government job, but with a high-value mindset. Everybody in the family are happy and appreciative of their simple lives. But Armaan feels his dreams can never fit in the box he lives in, nor can he fit in with these people. He has seen his father's counterparts living better lives, but all his father wants is for his son to be content, not taunt him the way he does.

One day Armaan asks his father for a bike, but gets to hear that he has to earn it – he has to work hard and get an MBA degree with a good score. He does, and on Diwali that year, his father, with his little resources, gets a second-hand scooter, paints it, and accessorises it with new and fancy-looking parts with immense love and pride. He even ties a red ribbon around it and covers it with new tarpaulin. In the evening when Armaan comes home to celebrate with his family, he gets excited to see the new tarpaulin and rushes to take it off, but the smile instantly turns into a frown. He storms to his room and starts packing his bag. He calls his father a shameless man who has not given a thing to his family. Everybody is stunned by his words. He says so many derogatory and disrespectful things that even his mother chooses her husband's dignity over the rude and uncouth son.

Armaan leaves his home that night. With the little money that he has and some earned through unfair dealings, he moves to Mumbai. Despite the person he has grown to be, he has inherited some qualities from his father which helps him get a job in an MNC. Promotions follow and very soon tables turn for him.

His boss, a wonderful man, is looking for a groom for his daughter, Meera. Armaan has always been kind and nice to him and Meera in order to win them over. Even though Meera is arrogant and spoilt, he has always been flirtatious with her because he knows how rich she can make him. And without any surprise, he is the first choice for both father and daughter. Armaan is in love with her money, but in his heart he still longs for Shraddha, a middle-class, graceful, warm, loving, and kind girl, whom he had dated once. Armaan, Arjun, Shraddha, and Jaswinder (Jassi) were inseparable childhood friends up until college. He had promised to marry Shraddha as soon as he made a life for himself. Instead Armaan chooses an empty and superficial life due to his greed for money. In all this, Arjun marries Shraddha.

After Armaan and Meera get married, he starts his own company and in addition is given the responsibility of his father-in-law's business. Life goes on; he has money, but no happiness or peace. His kids grow up to be arrogant and rude, and call their father uncultured and backward. He has never been able to build a stable and respectable image for himself as his children have always seen him dancing to their mother's tune. Armaan's mother-in-law also treats him like a small-town, filthy boy to whom they have done a favour. It feels like he has lost happiness and along with it, hope.

On a business trip to Delhi, he comes across his childhood friend Jassi on a flight. He is instantly transported to the days when he was happy. He notices a metal rod on Jassi's ankle and asks him about it. Jassi recounts that he served in the Indian Army where he was captured by the enemies and subjected to barbarity. When he managed to escape, he was shot in his legs. But by this time he had already run across the border into our country and was rescued. Even after losing both his legs, his spirit remained unbroken. He became the head of a security agency and has started giving motivational speeches.

This triggers a change in Armaan. He realizes that even with a full body and all possible luxuries, he is miserable. Jassi will be meeting Arjun for dinner and invites Armaan. Though ashamed of facing his friends after all these years and everything he did to them, he still agrees. Arjun and Shraddha are pleasantly surprised to see Armaan and welcome him without a trace of grudge. He sees how wholesome their life, with their two children, is and not for once does he feel jealous of their happiness.

The visit to his friends' place consumes his emotions. He misses his family and is reminded of his humble beginnings, of his father's funeral, the only time he visited home after abandoning his family. It was there he realized they have no love or space for him in their hearts any more. His presence at his father's funeral was worthless to them, as he was made aware of the decision that his younger brother would perform all rituals.

The night of his return to home after the business trip is Diwali. He decides to go back to his house and family that he had grown up detesting. Instead of going back home for the extravagant Diwali party, he heads to the old lanes that smell of his childhood.

Back home his wife is waiting for him. When she hears the doorbell, she opens it thinking it is Armaan. Instead, it is the driver who hands over a box – in it are his wedding ring, wallet, credit cards, property papers, divorce papers, and a note thanking her for all that she has given him and apologizes for leaving, for he has today realized that he has taken enough from her; it was time for him to give back and thus has decided to donate all his profits to NGOs.

He enters the lanes of his colony. Everybody is celebrating together. They are dumbfound at his sudden arrival, communicating disappointment through their eyes. His eyes land up on the scooter that started it all, still covered in the same tarpaulin, now old and covered with dust. He uncovers it, dusts it, and struggles to kick-start it. And when it does, he is overcome with joy. He hears the children pleading his brother to get them more crackers. Armaan smiles, '*Bacchon, aa jao. Chalo aaj bade papa pataake lekar denge.*' (Come kids, today your father's elder brother will get you firecrackers.) They look at their grandmother shyly, who in turn has the same look in her eyes. In the end of this wordless exchange, they break into a slight smile.

Armaan secretly wipes away a tear and takes off as the children hop on to his scooter.

Questions

Do we lose out on enjoying our lives while chasing the chimera of worldly success?

Can relationships be equated to wealth?

6
FIVE DESI AMERICANS

Four immigrants from diverse cultures set out for the Great American Dream. This is a story about how these four lives intersect at their landlord's house. The landlord, a Punjabi-Pakistani man at heart, finds his cultural roots once again in the crazy melting pot that his house has now become.

This isn't the story of a hero, everyone is a hero in a sense but only within the boundaries of the mediocrity of their ordinary life. Hence, there's no one character that triggers the beginning. All the four characters are equally important:

A free spirited, light hearted, naive and outlandishly silly (yet witty) Jatt Sikh boy from Punjab named Harjit. He crosses the Mexican border into America to fulfil his father's stubborn desire for him to marry an Indian-American Sikh girl, for he believes back in the days his own love was stolen from him by an NRI Jatt Sikh man. It is his idea of redemption that lands his son in America, illegally.

A clear hearted, compassionate and thoughtful Afghan whose circumstances threatened him out of Afghanistan called Ali.

A compliant and dutiful goody-two-shoes, who internally is just another young girl with the weight of responsibilites too heavy for her. Mansi belongs to a Brahmin household from Chennai and is visiting America on a tourist visa of one year. An Anglo-Indian Christian nurse who's been made to feel like she doesn't belong in her country.

There is also a lawyer, Miguel Gill. He is Mexican from his mother's side and Punjabi Jatt from the side of his father. He is 'ABCD', America Born Confused Desi. All his life, he has been shuffling identities because he does not completely fit in any one identity but has never settled with one as he feels like he can't completely fit into either of the three cultures.

Ali, the Afghan youth and Mr Khan, the landlord, find in the other what they have been missing in themselves. Ali finds a home and Mr Khan finds companionship. The fact that they are fellow Muslims makes it even more effortless for them to come together.

Soon after Ali has started living at Mr Khan's place, he meets Harjit as they strike up a conversation while sitting on a common park bench. Because of Harjit's endearing personality, Ali grows fond of him. When he learns that he needs an apartment, Ali brings him to Mr Khan's residence. Mr Khan objects on the basis of his religion as Harjit is a Sikh, but Ali vouches for him and also the fact that an additional tenant will mean additional income.

Ali works in an English-teaching centre for refugees. Harjit is about to begin his search for a job, when he realizes that he is illegal here and hence without a work permit. In this epiphanic moment, Ali suggests he wear his Afghani cap and draw a mole on his face to match his photograph in his work permit. They believe they can fool people and thereby find work. Armed with a work permit, Harjit soon starts working at a gas station owned by an Iranian. To counter the language problem, he pretends to be dumb.

Soon, Ali meets Mansi, the girl from Chennai. To meet her family's pressure of getting settled here and then bringing them over has brought Mansi to America on a tourist visa. She is nervous, but finds some confidence when she meets a lawyer, Miguel Gill, who suggests she find herself a job at a centre run by refugees and immigrants, the same place where Ali works. She meets Ali at the centre and expresses her desire to teach children. Her simplicity and struggle reminds him of his lost love, and he feels empathetic towards her. So he gives her the job. He cannot risk getting arrested because he is an immigrant and she will be working on a tourist visa, so he suggests she teach children at his place. Mansi spends her days living in shabby hostels in an equally shady environment, but seeks solace in teaching.

But tired of her living conditions, Mansi breaks down in front of Ali one day. Even though he wants to help her, Ali knows allowing a Tamil Brahmin woman in his residence will irk the landlord. But he is able to convince Mr Khan because he too can feel her pain. As a gesture of gratitude, Mansi offers to cook for them and help them as much as possible, and it takes no time for her to become part of the household.

Life sometimes puts you in unknown, unexpected situations. This one time at work one of the Muslim guys working at the gas station stops by the junkyard to take a piss. Harjit lands himself in a comical situation where seeing his mannerism his co-workers guess correctly that he is not circumcised and is a shame to the community. When he cannot deny, they even suggest to organize the ceremony for him the next day to make him 'a complete Muslim man'.

Harjit runs away and never returns to work. He then goes to Miguel, cussing all the way, and asks him to help him find a white girl. A few weeks later, Miguel introduces him to an American-born Punjabi girl. On seeing the girl's attitude who goes on cursing on the phone while stubbing out a cigarette, Harjit takes Miguel aside and tells him, '*Punjabiyaan de naa te kalank aa tu. Aa kiho jihi Punjaban labi aa saaleya?*' (You are a disgrace in the name of a Punjabi. What kind of a Punjabi girl have you got me here?) To Harjit, Miguel cannot justify his last name – Gill. He thinks he is having a conversation with a fellow Punjabi, but in return all he hears is gibberish from Miguel and gets even more confused.

It takes Harjit no time to find another job under Ali's name. This time he lands himself the job of a pizza delivery man which leads to some hilarious adventure. He cannot believe it when he lands up at a woman's house and she invites him to her bedroom. Excited and aroused, as soon as he gets into her bedroom she starts undressing. Harjit lands himself in yet another uncomfortable situation because the person turns out to be androgynous!

He is so used to Ali's identity now that he responds to the call of that name. Once when his father fixes him up with an NRI girl, he goes to meet her straight from work, without changing his cap or removing the fake mole. He even greets people with *assalam wallaykum*! Managing the dual identity becomes draining and even risky at times for him.

Tired of the pranks his life has been playing on him, he spends his energy into roaming around, flirting with girls, and trying to get them. One day, he comes across a pretty, white girl and catcalls her in Punjabi thinking she will not understand. To his horror, Lara responds equally harshly, swearing in crude Hindi, and almost beats him up. He has to spend a good while tendering his apology. She is frustrated and while swearing at him, mentions something about being homeless in this foreign land and having to deal with such men. On hearing this, Harjit feels that helping her find a place to live will redeem his actions. He introduces her to Mr Khan, who is not thrilled at all to see yet another guest! Harjit tries to argue that now Mansi can have a roommate.

Mr Khan does not refuse because he can do with the extra money. So he moves to the basement to provide space for all his guests. Four brown people, from extremely different cultures, living under one roof means a new festival every other week. Together they celebrate Eid, Diwali, Christmas, Gurupurab, and their birthdays. They find solace in each other, a shared sense of brokenness, separation and purpose. It brings a kind of bustle to Khan's life that makes him forget he was ever lonely or miserable.

Khan is middle-aged and has what all his tenants want – a house in America and citizenship. But what they have he does not – companionship. Time and again, he is reminded of his now-deceased wife on whom he spent all his savings to treat her of her cancer. And his son, whom he kicked out of the house when he came out as gay.

The tale of broken love is nothing new.

Ali's fiancée, back in his days in Afghanistan, wanted to teach young girls and give them the education they deserve. But this was not allowed in their country. She faced every challenge thrown her way with courage, but in the end was killed by the Taliban. This couple was especially targeted: while one wanted to empower women, the other, Ali, was a translator to the American soldiers at war. Since Ali had been loyal to them, the Americans decided to help him by granting him asylum in their country.

Similar circumstances brought Lara to this new land. She was accused of converting people and faced the ire of the extremist religious groups. While the others in the house faced enemies in their own country, Mansi has to face them from her own home. She is burderned with sponsoring them, especially her younger brother, to America.

Amidst these stories of misery is that of Harjit, which, like his persona, is a little serious than theirs.

There are now two legal and two illegal immigrants living in Khan's house. One day the white American immigration officer, Christy, pays them a visit. The others run around to hide Mansi in the kitchen and Harjit in the closet since they both think they will be caught and deported. But it turns out that she has come to inform Ali of the green card he is soon going to get. Before leaving she throws a nasty look at the mess they had created, perhaps thinking they are not capable of living in a civilized manner. Harjit is specifically scared out of his wits because he had once tried to woo her not realizing she is an immigration officer.

As it happened, Lara and Harjit fall in love. He starts transforming her into a Punjaban and it is hilarious to hear his words in her accent. One day, while he is on video call with his father, his father hears someone calling out to Harjit in Punjabi. He has to quickly handle the situation and get her dressed in a salwar suit to present her as his American girlfriend. Often there are funny episodes of his drunk father venting out at him and having a hilarious and silly man-to-man conversation. One of those times, he asks Harjit when he will bring him to 'Amreeka in his private jet'. Harjit, while he is sitting on the toilet seat, exclaims that everybody in his house has their own personal private jet!

Both Lara and Ali enjoy benefits over the two illegal immigrants. Whenever they need to get any work done, all they do is scare them by pretending to make a phone call to the immigration office to report the two illegal immigrants. Ali, who hates Harjit's lazy ways and lack of hygiene, gets irritated when Harjit throws his stinky socks at him. It is quite a humorous scene of Ali getting frustrated and scaring him to get him deported, all because of a rotten pair of socks.

But things take an unexpected turn when this joke turns into someone's reality. One day, there is a raid at Mansi's workplace and she is arrested and deported. Miguel tries very hard to prevent this, but every attempt fails. In the house, apart from Lara and Harjit, Mansi and Ali too care for each other deeply, albeit unexpressed. Ali sees in Mansi his lost love, and Mansi appreciates the kindness he showed her. When Mansi is sent back, Ali calls her up in India and hesitantly asks her to marry him. He has a Green Card holder now, which will help her come here and apply for a PR. Once she gets the PR, he will divorce her. Her selfish family agrees to this idea. Time flies without them confessing their love for each other. And as soon as Mansi gets her PR, her short-lived happiness that she had accidentally found is snatched from her when her family reminds her of the condition. With heavy hearts the couple parts ways, and Mansi's family marries her to her third cousin in order to get him to America. This man turns out to be an abusive partner, but she has no strength left in herself to retaliate. But one day she realizes that she is the one who brought him here and he cannot use her anymore, and she files charges against him. The couple is soon divorced.

She finally musters the courage to tell her family that she will not sponsor anybody with her future at stake. She informs them of her wish to remarry Ali, and only if they accept this can they come and live with her.

For Harjit and Lara, things proceed smoothly: Lara is granted PR after a year, and Harjit ends up fulfilling the purpose of his visit, but not just by marrying a Green Card holder, but by marrying the one he loves.

Mr Khan finally accepts his son the way he is and brings him back home.

Without trying or saying, just by following the path of love, the young lot end up teaching Khan a lesson to remember and cherish.

Questions

Do we create barriers in our mind about compatibility, family and friendships on the basis of our perception of culture as exclusive?

How can people retain their identities yet be tolerant towards others in multicultural situations?

7
CONNECTION

Aditya Sethi, a man in his mid-forties, works as a managing director in a big company. His wife, Renu, has a big gang of friends who meet very often and stay in touch over social media. Their children, Sanyam, seventeen, and Mitali, fourteen, are the budding youth of this tech-savvy world, addicted to the new world of technology. They live in Amritsar.

Aditya's mother (Dadi or grandma) is a religious person and can be mostly found with a mala[1] in her hand or performing puja. Though respected, she longs for the attention of the family, but has now adjusted to the times thinking *bachche khush rahein* (kids should be happy). Another neglected member of the family is Bruno, the golden retriever. He is petted only if they have time, but the faithful dog is always loving and happy with whatever attention he gets, just like Dadi. The full-time maid, Savita's head is always bowed, not as a sign of respect, but due to being engrossed in her mobile phone.

1 April 2018. It is a regular day in the Sethis household. Aditya's day starts with the usual tea, newspaper, and checking of business emails. He has to rush to the office because time is always short in this fast, stressful, hectic life and everyone is running in a race without a finishing line. Renu is ready for her social gathering and is too busy to give proper attention to her grown-up kids, who are also busy and happy without the interference from their mother. Savita is busy attending to her chores as well as her mobile phone. Twenty-four hours seem too short to some and too long to others.

2 April 2018. A call for bandh is announced across the state of Punjab due to the reservation matter of the Scheduled Castes and Scheduled Tribes. As a security measure, all media connections via mobile data are blocked by the government. Accidentally, Bruno has chewed off the WiFi wire the previous night, so even the home Internet connectivity is not available. The driver is sent to the market to buy new wire and get it installed, but because of the bandh, he is unable to get any.

The bandh disrupts the life of the Sethi household. Without the Internet, everyone is stressed. Bruno is cursed for chewing the wire, and even the government is not spared. However, soon everyone starts to calm down. With nothing else to do in their rooms, they all come out and sit in the lobby. It is a different scene in the house today. Everyone seems much relaxed.

Bruno is confused but happy because today everyone is playing with him and paying attention. Mitali and Sanyam, who usually get irritated with Dadi, are enjoying getting pampered by her. The maid too, without any distraction, has become more efficient. Renu, not able to go out with her friends, pays attention to the house. She sees dust on the furniture and things kept in an unorganized manner. She even cooks lunch for the family; Thai curry, her speciality. Aditya receives a call from his childhood friend, Rishab. They have only been in touch over text messages because they cannot spare time from their hectic routine to talk to each other. They talk about their simple yet happy past and decide to meet for dinner the same evening. He seems relaxed and far away from the daily chaos. Mitali is in the kitchen making chocolate cookies for everyone. Savita has been asked to churn out tea and pakoras, but she is not complaining because nothing is hindering her work. Dadi is surprised but happy and thinks her prayers for a united family have been answered, and so she goes to the puja room to thank her god.

Everyone is enjoying the attention they are paying to each other. They decide to see some old video recordings of the family, stashed away in an untouched box. Aditya misses his father when he sees these videos.

The kids demand to go on a long drive. Although they do not go on drives frequently, whenever they do, Dadi and Bruno are the happiest. As soon as a white sheet is spread on the last seat of their seven-seater SUV, Bruno understands it is for him and starts wagging his tail in excitement.

Everything is set for the evening. It is decided that they will leave at 7 p.m. for the drive, and then Aditya and Renu will meet Rishabh for dinner.

Dadi and Bruno are ready and waiting for everyone else. Suddenly, at 6.45 p.m., the Internet connection is restored. It is 7.10 p.m. and still no one turns up.

Renu usually takes about fifteen minutes to get ready, but is taking longer because she is answering tons of messages and emails which have piled up since the morning. Aditya knocks at her door, but she sounds irritated. 'You go ahead. What difference does it make if one member is missing from the drive?'

He then calls Savita, who answers on the third call. She emerges from the kitchen after disconnecting a phone call. He sends her to fetch Mitali who is on a Skype call with a friend from London. 'I need to call another friend in the US. What difference does it make if I can't go for the drive?'

Sanyam is annoyed when Aditya walks into his room without knocking. 'You have spoilt my mood and I no more wish to go with you, and it really doesn't matter if one person is absent from the drive.'

Seeing Aditya's expression, his mother understands what has happened. He goes to her and says, 'Let's go.' But she smiles, picks up her walking stick, and says, 'What difference does it make if we all don't go?' and walks to her room.

Savita asks Aditya if she should remove the cotton sheet from the back seat of the car. Aditya silently nods. Bruno is confused why the sheet is removed. He looks at Aditya with longing eyes and soon understands. To make up for the lost drive, he asks Savita to give Bruno the leftover chicken pieces from lunch.

Bruno becomes happy and content as before. Dadi is busy in her evening prayers. Savita is engaged in her kitchen chores. The others have transported into the virtual world. But Aditya is free. Not knowing what else to do, he switches on the mobile data and starts answering hundreds of unanswered messages and email.

Questions

Are our relationships in the immediate surroundings gradually dying?

Are we connected more to others through the virtual world than our own family members?

8
THE OTHER SIDE

A rich Sindhi family finally manages to get their Pakistani visas after a long wait. Hemant Vasvani is an established businessman residing in a posh colony of Mumbai. He owns a textile trading company. He wants to visit the historical Sikh shrines, especially Guru Nanak's birthplace, Nankana Sahib, now across the border, along with his wife, Sunita, and their twenty-three-year-old son, Vaibhav, who has just finished his textile designing course.

Hemant's friend, Basheer Khan, a textile supplier and owner of a big textile unit, helps him get the visa. Basheer is Hemant's business associate and close friend living in Lahore and belonging to an influential family. He lives there with his wife, Mariyam, and their twenty-one-year-old daughter, Nafisa, who is pursuing a course in fashion designing. It is decided that Hemant and his family will stay with Basheer during their seven-day visit.

Although Basheer and Hemant have been associated for a long time, it is the first time the families are meeting.

Mariyam and Basheer give them a warm welcome and make them comfortable in their palatial house. From the very first day Vaibhav and Nafisa get along well because of their common interests as well as the common subject of their studies. Nafisa accompanies Vaibhav's family to every visit to the shrines. She is a humble girl and is praised by Hemant, Sunita, and Vaibhav alike. Vaibhav develops a strong attraction for Nafisa, but does nothing about it thinking it is a short trip and they will get back to their own lives once he leaves.

The seven days come to an end and Hemant's family leaves for India with fond memories and new friendships. Vaibhav and Nafisa, and Sunita and Mariyam, keep in touch.

A few months later, Hemant's niece's wedding is going to take place in Udhampur. He invites Basheer and his family because of his close association, but also because Nafisa had earlier expressed her wish to see an Indian wedding. They are all excited to visit India for the wedding.

The festivities bring the two families even closer. Vaibhav and Nafisa spend hours dancing and talking, and finally confess their feelings for each other. To them, coming from different religions or even country did not matter. But this very reason causes much worry to the two families and they stand against their relationship. The children try to convince their families to accept them, but they remain adamant in their decision and refuse any further discussion on the topic.

Suddenly, relations and feelings towards each other change. Basheer blames Vaibhav for influencing his daughter, while Hemant starts disliking Nafisa thinking her to be oversmart. But Vaibhav and Nafisa believe their relationship can survive, and take a stand that they will be together even if the families disapprove.

Basheer returns to Lahore with his family the next day. But it seems Vaibhav and Nafisa have different plans: they plan to elope from Amritsar when Basheer's family cross the border into their country. Nafisa accompanies her parents to Amritsar, while Vaibhav arrives there through a different route. Minutes before crossing the border, Nafisa excuses herself to use the restroom.

Time passes and Nafisa does not return, leaving her parents worried. Everyone is frantically looking for her, but Nafisa is nowhere to be found. Basheer suddenly believes that she has fled with Vaibhav. Through his high contacts, he registers a case against Vaibhav. The incident catches media attention and within no time the news goes viral. On the other hand, Basheer and Mariyam have no choice but to return to their country because their visa has now expired. Nafisa's visa has also expired. The young couple applies in court for marriage and a blanket bail wherein they mention that they are adults and their actions are being taken in full consciousness, and that Nafisa has run away from home with her will.

Back in Lahore, Basheer hires a lawyer to argue that his daughter will now be forced to change her religion. But Vaibhav, who is fighting the case himself, answers that it is not his intention. Earlier he was agnostic, but looking at the games people are playing it has lifted any faith he remotely ever had in god. Nafisa, a believer of Sufi ideology, argues that there is only one creator teaching the same lesson.

Vaibhav further delves into history and brings forth the fact that centuries ago, people were not divided by religion, but the negativity of a few people turned the tables and divided the country based on religion. Even Einstein had to leave his country, Germany, when faced with such a divide, and considered this to be a threat in his own country. Vaibhav says he does not want this future for them where fear forces them to settle in a different country.

The judge, a rationalist by nature, is impressed by this young man's reasoning. He appeals to the public that religion, which stabilizes the minds and is seen as a ray of hope for many, should not act as a barrier. He clears any and all charges against the idealistic Vaibhav and approves of their union.

The parents are helpless in the court ruling and surrender to the wishes of their children. Vaibhav and Nafisa get married with the blessings of their parents.

Questions

Why do we create so many hindrances and barriers for people of two communities or two countries to be together?

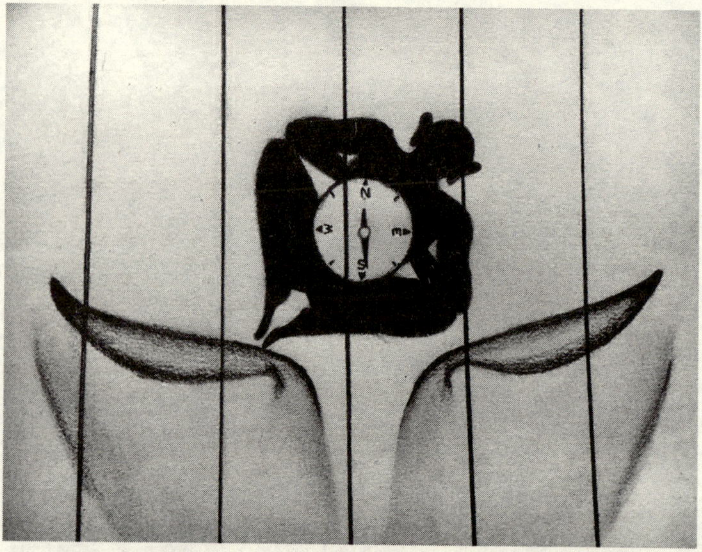
N
S

9

VASTU SHASTRA

After completing his studies from a small town, Saurabh, a chartered accountant, gets a job in an MNC in Mumbai. He is religious and to some extent superstitious by nature.

He moves to the city with his wife, Shalini, and his eight-year-old son, Rahul. Early years of hard work and discipline earns him a lot of respect at work. In a short time, he earns sufficient to invest in an apartment. They plan to move in to their new home in a couple of months. Shalini and Saurabh want their new life to be smooth, so they plan to seek the help of a vastu expert.[1] The whole discussion is carried out in front of Rahul, an intelligent, observant, and inquisitive child, which raises a series of questions in his mind.

The following day Saurabh makes an appointment with a vastu expert to meet at their new apartment. But this expert tells Saurabh that he should have discussed everything before buying the property; he knows a builder who had recently built two towers of twenty-seven floors each at his advice and supervision specially for the vastubelieving clients, for which they had to just pay an extra five per cent. But Saurabh explains that this apartment is near his relative's place and being near his office it will save him commute time. The vastu expert then starts to talk about positive and negative, more of negative, energies flowing into each room, tells them how to place the furniture, and even advises them to demolish and rebuild certain parts of their apartment.

The whole time Rahul is carefully listening and is becoming more and more curious. As soon as his father pauses, young Rahul interrupts: How does one calculate the enormous amount of energy of the sun, coming from trillions of miles away, into a small room of a small apartment? How is it decided which corner gets what amount of energy? How can one determine whether the energy is positive or negative?

His questions leave the expert stunned and displeased, but replies calmly, '*Bachche abhi tum bahut chhote ho, tum nahin samajh paaoge. Iske peechhe science aur bahut si calculations hain.*' (Child, you are too young to understand these things. There's science and many calculations behind this.)

Suddenly, Rahul is all excited, '*Uncle, mere favourite subjects science aur mathematics hain aur main bada hoke scientist banna chahta hoon. Isliye poochh raha hun ki aap yeh calculations kaise karte hain. Yeh to zaroor bahut hi interesting naya calculation method hoga*' (Uncle, science and mathematics are my favourite subjects and I want to become a scientist when I grow up. For this reason I am asking you how these calculations are done. This sure must be an interesting new method of calculation.)

Rahul's parents are surprised. Unable to answer even one of his questions, the expert is embarrassed.

Suddenly, the vastu expert receives a call. '*Kya kahaa? Ma seediyon se gir gayi? Tum ambulance bulao, main jaldi pahunchta hun!*' (What? Mother has fallen from the stairs? You call the ambulance, I'm reaching at once!) He rushes out of their apartment.

But the child's thirst for knowledge is not quenched yet. He turns to his parents. '*Kya Uncle ne apne ghar mein seediyan vastu ke according nahin banvayi jo unke ghar mein yeh mishap ho gaya?*' (Did Uncle not get the stairs in his home built according to vastu that this accident took place?)

The parents are left with a series of questions in their adult minds.

Questions

Why do we blindly believe in remedies where the basis of these practices cannot be determined?

Does Rahul bring any questions to your mind too?

10

UMMIDEIN – A LIFE OF DESIRES

This is a story of a boy, born into an upper-middle-class family after two daughters, living in a big city. Family and peer pressure do not allow him to lead a normal life and so he decides to leave his family for good at the age of twenty-seven. This story is narrated by him.

Today I'm a little over three weeks and I hear my heartbeat for the first time. Before this I was only a piece of flesh with no signs of life. But now I have a heart which beats with the first breath of life. I have become a human being not yet born. A human being is 'considered' superior to other species on earth, but the real problem starts now with the development of my brain. I can now feel hunger, pain, discomfort in my mother's womb.

I am growing up fast. I have started to differentiate between happy and sad voices, judging by their tone. I feel happy when I hear my mother's soothing voice sing me a lullaby. I feel scared when someone is crying or shouting. I feel discomfort when I hear sad voices.

I am twenty-weeks-old today. I can feel the pressure on my body, especially below the naval, which lasted only a few minutes, but my gentle body is aching because of this mild pressure. I now hear two or three happy voices. I had never heard so much joy in these voices before and this makes me forget my pain.

I am born today. After crying for a while, with great difficulty I open my eyes and find the world upside down. The first impression of this world is strange. I am confused to see grown-up humans standing on their heads without any support. Only after half a minute, the doctors bring me to the normal position. Ah, now my head is up and feet down.

I see my two elder sisters looking at me with love, and my father, with great pride. The nurses ask my father for money for fathering a boy. He happily gives them some, but they want more because I am born after two daughters. Now I understand why I had felt the pain below my naval when I was just twenty-weeks-old. I understand that I am a privileged member of this family.

I can hear my mother speak. 'He is my diamond.'

Father: '*Mere budhape ka sahara*' (My support in old age.)

Dadi:[1] '*Beheno ka rakhwala aagaya*' (The protector of his sisters.)

Elder sister: '*Ab main bhi rakhi bandhungi aur mujhe bhi paisa milega*' (I can now tie a rakhi and get money.)

Younger sister to elder sister: '*Didi, ab main iske saath khelungi aur daantungi bhi jab yeh shararat karega kyunki main ab tumhari daant nahin sunne wali*' (Didi, I can now play with him and even scold him, because I am now not going to listen to your scoldings.)

Hearing this, everyone is laughing, but I am a little worried. No one has asked me what I will do with my life!

Time passes. I am pampered, but expectations from me rise each day.

I am a twenty-seven-year-old, educated, handsome man now. Both my sisters are married. My mother is a homemaker who does everything perfectly, as is expected of all good Indian housewives. My father is a happy man. Business is settled and I am working hard and have taken the responsibilities of the factory on my shoulders. Dadi is very sick and wants to see me married soon and prays to god to give her more time to see her great grandchildren.

My parents have found a rich girl for me. I requested to meet her first to see if our interests match. They could then organize a small family meeting to finalize our *rishta*.[2] I am waiting for her in a coffee shop for our first meeting. She enters – fair, tall, long hair. I am happy to see her and have almost made up my mind even before talking to her. She smiles and sits before me. We talk about our interests, hobbies, movies, clothes, places, foods.... Surprisingly, our likes and dislikes are similar!

I then ask about her expectations from her husband.

She replies: 'You have touched upon a sensitive topic, but it is important I answer with honesty because this will be the foundation for our happy married life. I wish my husband understands all my hidden wishes and feelings which were suppressed by my only elder brother. My family, especially my parents, have always ignored my desires. We were not rich, so all his wishes were fulfilled at the cost of mine during my childhood years. I want my husband to fulfil all my wishes which were lost during my upbringing.'

I draw a blank. Unable to respond, I ask her for permission to leave telling her I am not feeling well. She is worried and offers help, but I leave.

Instead of going home, I go to a friend's house. Both he and his wife work together in an advertising company. I have the keys to his house and am allowed entry whenever I want some alone time while they are away. I come here to pour out my emotions on paper, feel relaxed, tear off the pages, and go back to routine life.

Today, I am sitting at the writing desk and writing for the last time, but this time the words with my emotions will reach where they should reach and not get trashed.

Dear family,

Papaji, till now, I have tried to fulfil all your wishes as best as I could, but I cannot continue any further.

Mamma, your unconditional love has made me more emotional, but this unconditional love also has one hidden reason: to love you back with full fervour and to remain a mamma's boy. But now I am a grown-up man and want to make my own path.

Dadi, you loved me more than you loved my sisters, I am thankful, but I will not be able to fulfil your last wish of seeing my children. You can happily die because your last wish has already been fulfilled by your granddaughters. You should not differentiate between your pota *and* potis.[3]

I cannot marry the girl of your choice because she too expects me to fulfil her desires. I am unwilling to bear the burden of new expectations. All these years, I have some unfulfilled desires and expectations from my own self, and I will try to fulfil these now.

I am leaving this city, and do not know when I will ever return. The world is not a nice place, but I must leave to find myself. My friend Vikas is aware of my whereabouts, but please do not force him to reveal this – I have warned him that he will lose a friend if he does this for you. I'm sure I'll return one day, but until then you need to realize that it is not the duty of the son to fulfil everyone else's dreams and expectations.

Take care until then.

Your not-so-sincere son,

Vijay

Before meeting this girl, Vijay had gone to watch a movie with a friend, *Dil Dhadakne Do*. He realizes his heart was never allowed to beat.

Questions

Is it alright to project our desires on other people for their fulfilment?

In the story, the daughters are affected finally by the primacy given to the son and the son feels the impact of expectations on him. How can these be balanced in our society to not pressurise the next generation?

11

STREET HOOKER

Pushpa, a twenty-eight-year-old slum dweller, is standing, decked out in a bright pink saree and accessorized fully, in the dark corner of a street, waiting for her fate in the shape of a client, who will pay her to use her body, so that she can go home and feed her children. Another four or five women are also standing at a distance, not willing to snatch each others' clients, awaiting the same fate.

Pushpa could not fetch a client the previous day. So, she is desperate to find one today. The others have already found theirs, but she is still waiting. Just then a car stops in front of her and the window is rolled down. Pushpa is surprised to see the person inside the car. She has been noticing him from the last six days: he would pick a different woman each night. She asks him tauntingly, '*Kyun, jawaan, aaj meri baari?*' (Is it my turn today, young man?) He smiles. '*Do ghante ka kya logi?*' (What's your rate for two hours?)

Pushpa, considering this an opportunity, quotes five hundred rupees more than her usual price. To her surprise, the young man agrees. She sits in his car and they drive off. He introduces himself as Naresh.

The hotel Naresh takes her to is unlike what she has been taken to by her earlier clients. They walk to their pre-booked room. Naresh makes her sit on the sofa and Pushpa starts undressing and talking dirty. But Pushpa is surprised when he asks her to stop. '*Aur kya chahta hai?*' (What else do you want?)

Naresh tells her slowly that he does not want her body. Pushpa is confused now. In typical street language, she tells him, '*Time khotti mat kar, jis liye laya hai woh kaam kar.*' (Don't waste time. Do what you have brought me for.) But when Naresh refuses her body once again, she says, '*Phir paise kis baat ke?*' (What are you giving me money for then?) She gets up and starts to walk out of the room.

Naresh clarifies that he has paid her for her time, never once did he say that he is paying for her body. He then tells her that he is a social activist and journalist, researching prostitutes and making others aware of their miserable lives through his articles. Naresh sits next to Pushpa and very politely asks about her past, what brought about this ugly present. Pushpa is touched. For the first time ever a man is interested to learn about her agony.

They were a family of five: Pushpa, her husband, Rajnath, their two children, and her bedridden mother-in-law. They were poor and lived in the slums. Rajnath had been working as a sewer cleaner under a contractor of the municipal corporation for which he was paid two-fifty to three hundred rupees depending on the work. He loved his family a lot and never let Pushpa work for money despite their tight financial circumstances. He somehow managed to provide basic needs to his family.

There was a time when Rajnath had not been able to work for two days because he was unwell. He received a call from the contractor, who knew he needed the money, and offered him two hundred rupees to clean a sewer. By then Rajnath was feeling somewhat better, so he requested to be paid in full. But the contractor acted as if he was doing Rajnath a favour and said that he could hire another cleaner in the said amount. In desperate need of money, Rajnath agreed. Pushpa tried to stop him because he had not recovered completely, but he did not pay heed: there was not a single penny in the house, not even for the meal that night.

Little did he know it was the call of death. Rajnath lowered himself into the sewer without the required safety equipments, as it generally happens here. He choked to death due to the poisonous gases inside the sewer.

Pushpa was shocked to hear of her husband's death. She became so numb that not even a drop of tear fell from her eyes. All she could think about were the expenses, as Rajnath's body lay before her. With no one else to approach, she pleaded the contractor for compensation, but he refused saying it was not his responsibility. She then asked him to lend her some money in return for working under him once the death rituals were complete. Shamelessly, he said that the only job he had for her was to use her for which he was ready to pay an amount right away as also in future whenever she needed money. Left with no other option, Pushpa agreed and got the money she needed.

Finally the time came when Pushpa had to surrender herself to the contractor. The need for money erupted time and again: the two children had to be fed and the ailing mother-in-law had to be looked after. This led to her exploitation initially at the hands of the contractor and then by others, eventually leading her to her present profession.

Naresh is shaken. Pushpa's story has left him frustrated and remorseful.

Questions

Are the sewage cleaners in India exploited at the cost of their safety?

Who is responsible for their deaths while at work?

Should their families receive compensation on their death?

12

SHARPSHOOTER

Over the last two years, many social reformers, activists and rationalist writers speaking against superstitions and fanatics, are being murdered in India and Bangladesh. Earlier, such rationalists were honoured, such as Bhagat Singh, Subhas Bose and Jawaharlal Nehru, among many others. Some of the recent killings of social activists like M. M. Kalburgi, Gauri Lankesh, Santanu Bhowmik, are heart-rending. This story is about a renowned, professional sportsman, who cleverly saves a rational social activist and his own daughter from the clutches of conspirators.

Bhushan Bhardwaj, the leader of Seva Dal, a fundamentalist religious organization based in Bengaluru, is a powerful, corrupt, rigid, and fanatic leader.

Hari Krishnan, a social activist, is quite vocal about, and fights against the caste system and superstitions prevalent in the society, and has also filed a public interest litigation or PIL to implement anti-superstition laws in the state.

Ali, a renowned long-range shooting champion, has won many medals at national and international levels. He has a fourteen-year-old daughter, Sarah. His wife, Zoya, had gone from Bengaluru to Gujarat in 2002 to attend a wedding and she had been killed in the Gujarat riots along with her parents and brother. Ali was shattered, but had to strengthen himself for Sarah. Being a practical person, Ali has never developed hatred towards any community despite going through such a tragedy. He believes the mob killed them, and that mob and death have no religion. Ali has a dependable friend, Rahul, who lives nearby and they are really close to each other.

Ali is a very caring father. To compensate for the loss of her mother, Ali devotes ample time to Sarah. He comes back home from work every afternoon so that he can spend time with her when she returns from school. One afternoon Ali is a little late. When he reaches home, he is surprised to learn that Sarah has not yet returned from school. He calls up her school, but the office had closed by then. He starts to get worried when Sarah does not return even after waiting for an hour. He is about to leave to look for her when his mobile phone rings. An unknown number flashes across the screen. Negative thoughts cross his mind. Sarah has indeed been kidnapped, but the caller does not want ransom.

The caller is Bhushan Bhardwaj. In exchange of Sarah's release, he wants Ali to kill Hari Krishnan, who has become a threat to the preachings and activities of his political party.

Bhardwaj has chosen Ali for the assassination because of the latter's reputation as a sharpshooter. He threatens to kill his daughter if the work does not get done.

Hearing his daughter crying and pleading to save her, Ali feels trapped. He does not want to kill an innocent person, yet he has to save his daughter. Bhardwaj instructs him to go outside his house, walk till the end of the road where a dustbin was kept, throw his mobile phone into this dustbin, turn right and walk around twenty steps where he will find a mobile phone, and pick it. Ali does as instructed. The new phone rings and Bhardwaj tells him the plan for the murder. Krishnan leaves his house at 10 p.m. for a walk in the park every night after dinner. Ali is instructed to go to the park around 8.30 that evening to survey a spot from where he can take his shot. Bhardwaj also tells him he will be in touch with his brother and Ali over a conference call. His brother will follow Krishnan and confirm the killing, following which Sarah will be released. The assassination would take place the following night, and Ali has to reach the park an hour before Krishnan's arrival.

Ali goes to the park that evening. He watches a chowkidar strolling around the area, and waits for Krishnan to arrive at his designated time and watches him keenly. He decides the spot – the top of a water tank – a secluded, blind turn, from where he will shoot Krishnan.

He goes back home and cannot sleep the whole night.

The following night Ali reaches as per Bhardwaj's instructions. The chowkidar is sleeping on a bench and his mobile phone is lying by his side. Ali quietly picks up the phone and reaches his spot. Using the chowkidar's phone, he sends Rahul a text message alerting him of the situation. He tells him that he wants to save Krishnan and Sarah, and, at the same time, also expose the corrupt party leader. He tells Rahul to get metal bonding agent, which he has at home because of his trade, and seal all outlets of Krishnan's house. He then instructs his brother to dress up like Krishnan, in a white kurta pyjama, wrap a beige stole around his neck, and wear headphones and arrive at the park at 10 p.m. Rahul does as instructed immediately. Finding the main gate to Krishnan's house locked from inside, he jumps over it and pours the bonding agent on the door handles and the main lock on the gate.

Back in the park, the conference call between Bhardwaj, his brother, and Ali starts. Exactly at 10, Rahul, dressed as Krishnan, enters the park and begins his routine walk. Bhardwaj's brother begins to follow Rahul, all the while maintaining distance. On his third round, when he reaches the blind turn, he shifts to his right and runs back. Ali takes his aim and shoots, not at Krishnan/Rahul, but at Bhardwaj's brother. No sound is heard; the rifle had a silencer.

Rahul reaches the dead body, picks up his phone, and says '*Ho gaya*' (It's done.) He disconnects the call. Before leaving, using the same mobile phone, he types out a message claiming himself to be Bhushan Bhardwaj and that he has killed the activist Hari Krishnan, and uploads it on social media.

Ali now calls up Bhardwaj to release his daughter, but the cunning man says he will wait for his brother to return with a confirmation of Krishnan's death. This makes Ali very angry and he threatens to shoot his brother, who is still in range, if he does not release his daughter immediately. Bhardwaj gets scared and releases Sarah. Being the intelligent girl she is, Sarah runs to a nearby shop and calls up the police.

Bhardwaj informs Ali of his daughter's release and demands to see his brother now. Ali tells him that he has been sent to his rightful place and soon he too would sent there.

Meanwhile, until now trapped in his own house, Hari Krishnan successfully breaks open the seal and is about to step out for his night walk when he sees the news: *Hari Krishnan shot dead outside his house.* A shocked Krishnan jumps over the sealed main gate to see the milling crowd.

Seeing Krishnan alive, all cameras now point at the dead man's face. The headline changes to: *Seva Dal leader Bhushan Bhardwaj's brother shot dead.*

Seeing the news, Bhardwaj is furious and threatens to get Ali arrested for his brother's murder. But Ali is smart and had taken very calculated steps. The mobile he had been using was registered under the politician's name, and he had been recording their calls from the previous day. There is ample proof who the real killer is.

Bhardwaj is helpless. He lights a cigarette against the backdrop of police sirens, now getting closer and louder.

Questions

Why have we become so intolerant towards the secular and rational voices, who are merely questioning and challenging our age-old beliefs irrelevant in today's times?

Unable to answer these questions with logic, is silencing them by murder the solution?

NOTE BAN

13
NOTEBANDI

Savitri is an eighty-year-old widow living by herself in a tier-three city. She does not have a family: her husband died long back and she does not have children because she is a *baanjh.*[1] Her sole possession is a small double-storey house, the upper floor of which she has rented out. She has been surviving on her husband's meagre pension and the rent. Her tenant, Ramesh, is a cunning, middle-aged man, who pretends to be honest and loving towards Savitri. He pays a mere 1,250 rupees per month as rent, and does not pay for electricity and water. Instead, with his money, he indulges in bad habits such as drinking and spending on women. He even eats at Savitri's house. But Savitri does not mind because she considers him like the son she never had.

With age Savitri's eyesight and hearing are getting affected, so much so that she is not able to perform daily chores properly. In 10s, 20s, 50s, and 100s she has saved around 45,000 rupees to buy herself a hearing aid and get a cataract surgery done.

Overnight, the government announces *notebandi.*[2] Ramesh loses his job. He has one lakh rupees with him in denominations of 500 and 1,000 freshly collected as bribe from a client. Not knowing what to do, he decides to leave for his hometown. Unaware of this, Savitri tells Ramesh that she fears for her life: she has a lot of money in small denomination which she needs to keep safe. She is however unaware that 500 and 1,000 rupee notes are now banned. She also innocently tells him that she needs a lakh for her operation and hearing aid.

Ramesh's cunning mind suddenly spins a web. He tells Savitri that he can get her small currency notes changed for 500s and 1,000s, which will be easier for her to handle. He also suggests her to sell her bangles to gather the remaining money she needed. He convinces her to do this immediately since he is leaving for his hometown, and there will be nobody to take care of her. Savitri agrees. He takes her 45,000 rupees and gold bangles, and the very next day hands her the one lakh in 500s and 1,000s. He solves his problem illegally in this manner.

Savitri is very happy and thankful to Ramesh as she thinks he has helped her a lot. Innocently, she asks Ramesh to let her know if he finds another good tenant like himself, who can give her six months' rent in advance to secure her monthly expenses.

Ramesh replies with a mischievous smile: 'Don't worry, Amma! *Is desh mein bahut se achhe insaan hain mere jaise. Aur bhagwan ek na ek insaan aapke liye zaroor bhej dega jaise usne mujhe bheja tha.'* (There are many good souls in this country like me. God will definitely send someone along for you, like he sent me.)

Questions

Does money mean everything? How do we take care of our senior citizens?

How does a person's inner conscience allow them to do such a heartless act to an innocent, helpless person?

14

HUMANITY

Akram and Mohsin are good friends. Akram is the more religious of the two. He keeps a beard and follows all rituals like a true Muslim. Mohsin, on the other hand, is a clean-shaven, happy-go-lucky person with a broad view of the world, reflected in his thinking. It has been six months since college ended, and they are meeting today for the last time before Akram goes off to the Middle East to find himself a job. The friends are reminiscing their college days and all that they had done in the last six months.

Mohsin asks why Akram chose the Middle East, to which the latter replies that he wants to be with his brethren. He has high hopes that the rich Arabs there would definitely help their underprivileged brothers from poorer nations. Mohsin, being the rationalist, tries to clarify. '*Muslims achhe aur non-Muslims bure nahin hote, balki achhe aur bure insaan hote hain jo har kahin hote hain. Sab mulkon mein, sab shehron mein, aur sab jagahon par.*' (It's untrue that Muslims are good and non-Muslims, bad. Instead, there are good and bad people, and they are everywhere. In every country, every city, every place.) But Akram is stubborn and does not want to argue. He asks Mohsin about his future. Mohsin has applied for a job in Germany and is waiting for the call. After a long chat both friends part happily to begin their respective journeys.

Five years have passed.

Mohsin is now a rich, successful German national. He is visiting India on a business trip and is accompanied by his beautiful, hijab-wearing, German wife, a Muslim of Egyptian descent, and his two-year-old son. While his wife has taken their son for sightseeing, Mohsin returns to the hotel after a business meeting. He orders his meal and is relaxing when someone knocks at his door. Expecting it to be room service, he opens the door, but is shocked to see Akram! Akram with a tray in his hands. He is dressed as a hotel staff. He has shaved off his beard, a marker of his religion back in the days. Akram too is surprised to see the well-dressed Mohsin, now with a beard. He thinks the beard, similar to what he used to have, has enhanced Mohsin's personality.

Mohsin is overjoyed to see his old friend. He seats him in his room and they begin talking. Mohsin tells him about his life in Germany, how he met a German girl, fell in love, and married her within a year of shifting there, and that they have a son now.

Mohsin then asks Akram about his life and how he has now become a waiter at this hotel. Akram begins his story. After they parted ways five years back, he went to Oman where he worked as a labourer for a rich Muslim Sheikh who owned the construction company. The Sheikh had made him sign a five-year labour contract forcibly and had impounded his passport. He had no rights to marry there, could not be a citizen, had to pay heavy taxes, and was exploited. He ran back to his country as soon as the contractual period got over. With wet eyes he tells Mohsin that he has realized there are only good or bad humans, not good or bad Muslims.

Questions

What remains of faith when it gets shattered?

Is it that the Western world has more religious freedom to allow a non-believer to turn religious?

TAX
GST
SURCHARGES

15
GST

Four young men, Ashish, Rakesh, Akram, and David, all in their late twenties are small-time entrepreneurs. They make their living by going door-to-door selling cosmetics, accessories, daily needs items, small home appliances, and such like. Their infrastructure is so small that they are not even equipped with computers or additional staff; they do everything themselves. They are hard-working men, struggling day and night to earn not only for themselves, but also for their families back home in the villages. Despite all the efforts, they earn around fifteen to twenty thousand rupees per month. Out of this they pay rent, pay for transportation, food, and pay their bills, and also send some money back home.

Their businesses have become sluggish after the implementation of the GST, the Goods and Services Tax. Their clients, all rich and educated people, who buy from them because of the convenience of door-to-door and quick delivery services, now want GST bills. But they have never had the need to provide these before.

With the recent changes, these young businessmen are hesitant to produce such bills: declaring their trade margins in the IT department would mean to pay tax from their already meagre income; hiring additional staff would mean paying them salaries; buying more equipments would mean more money.

They are already spending their entire day outside, buying and selling their products. With the advent of online shopping, many clients have switched to digital technology and buy directly from the likes of Amazon, Flipkart, and Ebay. All four are worried as this has made survival difficult. How will they meet their daily expenses, pay bills or rent, and feed their families back home?

Rakesh, Akram, and David are sitting in Akram's small rented room one evening. Ashish has brought a bottle of whisky: he has the habit of taking a couple of pegs daily. Akram and David drink occasionally, but Rakesh is a teetotaller and is sitting quietly nibbling peanuts. Ashish suggests Rakesh to write a letter to the government and gets him a sheet. Rakesh begins:

Subject: Hamaare mann ki baat (What's on our mind)

We are ready to pay income tax and GST, but in this transition phase, we small-scale businessmen, cannot survive. So 'social security' is the need of the hour.

Be ready to feed our families.

Treat our illnesses.

Get our sisters and daughters married.

Because you have snatched 'jugaad' from us, something the low- and middle-income businesses were surviving on. The big companies with brand recognition, which buy items cheap and in bulk, pose a tough competition for us, but jugaad is the only system through which we face this tough challenge. Our survival, not being possible without jugaad, we demand social security for our families. Only then can we come under the GST ambit. Else we are bound to fail in this new corporate tax system.

India is a poor nation where the government has not done much for its people. A large part of this huge population, crammed in a small area, had been surviving on their jugaad skills as nothing was done by the government. Now if you snatch this from us, be prepared to feed almost 50 per cent of the population which is breathing hard to survive on their own.

They finish the letter, but when it comes to mentioning the name and address of the sender, they all back out. Soon they doze off. The letter stays there on the table along with the empty glasses and leftovers.

Next morning, they get ready in a haste and leave for work. The maid comes to clean the room. She picks up the letter, reads part of it, and throws it in the dustbin along with the empty bottles and packets of snacks.

Questions

Is it right for the government to impose laws without analysing the actual condition of people?

If so then why does it not provide any social security during the transition phase?

Why are the people left on their own to bear the brunt of abruptly implemented laws?

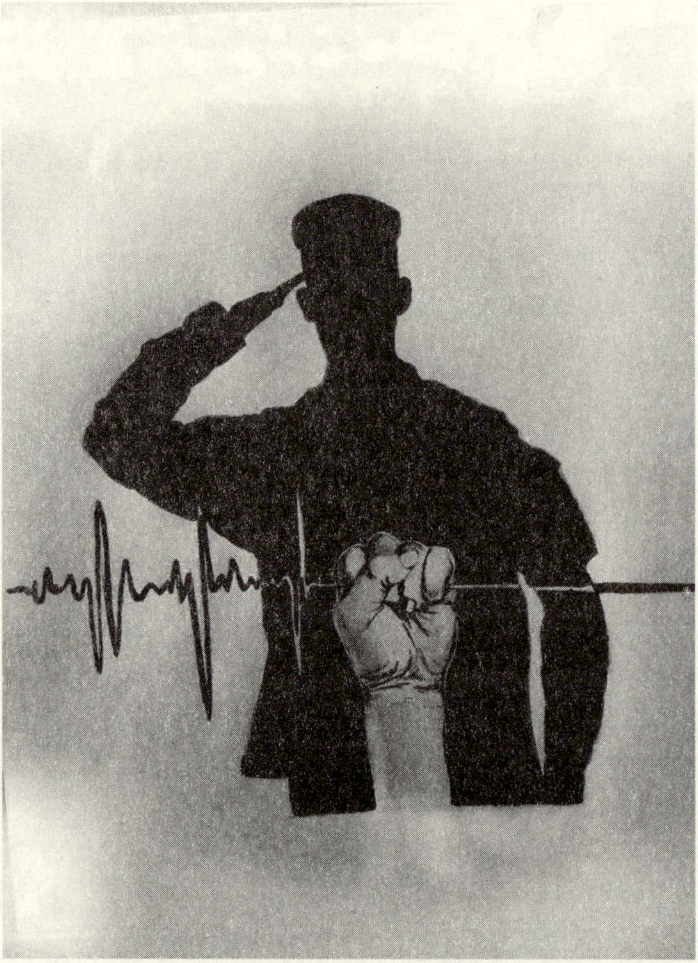

16

A LETTER TO THE PRESIDENT

Colonel Rathore, a sixty-year-old army officer, retired after losing his right arm following a grenade attack on his troops in the Northeast of India. Though a part of his body is injured, his spirit remains unharmed: he is as zestful and full of life as ever. His basic principles of life are dignity and respect. Despite his disability, he runs an NGO for poor children, and teaches them to live with self-respect and die a dignified death with peace of mind. His perspective of life is not to be dependent on anybody. Ever.

His wife died of cancer. In her last days, his main motive was to minimize her suffering. Thus he used morphine patches on her back to ease the pain. When he knew that there was no treatment left for her, he brought her home and gave her sedatives, so she could die peacefully in her sleep. He has a twenty-five-year-old unmarried daughter, who is a law-abiding Superintendent of Police.

One day while at the NGO, he suffered a stroke that left his lower body paralysed. With one arm less and a paralysed body, he is now confined to the bed. So much is his agony that he is unable to perform even basic, daily activities with his functional left hand. He is getting irritable with every passing day. Out of embarrassment he creates a lot of fuss when anyone else attends to his bodily requirements. In extreme cases his daughter ties the adult diaper herself, which makes him even more uncomfortable.

He pleads with his daughter to administer the lethal injection, to allow him a dignified death. But each time she refuses as it is illegal and does not want to go against the law. He tries to convince her each day. 'We army men are trained and taught to end our lives in war, in case we are unable to move or are critically injured, so that the enemy does not catch us alive and extract information, since it is a disgrace to our country to fall in the hands of the enemy'. He tells her that his soul is like his country and his disability, his enemy, and does not want his country to be disgraced by his enemy. He feels trapped and wants to free his soul from this disgrace. But his daughter remains adamant.

He calls his student, a commando who considers the colonel his mentor, personally very close to him. He requests him to come with his personal weapon and give it to him to end his undignified, disgraceful condition. But he too refuses.

Left with no other option, he writes a letter to the president of India, the chief of all three armed forces, to send his trained commandos and order a surgical strike to relieve his body from this disgrace and free his soul. It will be a disgrace to let a soldier die in helplessness and disgrace. He demands it as his fundamental right as a soldier. He also mentions that he does not want to commit suicide to end his agony as it will be a cowardly act. He is not a coward.

He ends his letter thus:

Awaiting your 'deadliest' reply at the earliest.

Question

Should euthanasia, or any such process, be allowed for those in a paralyzed state?

APPROVED
VISA

17
8 BANDS

Vishal, a thirty-four-year-old electrical engineer from a small town in Rajasthan, waits at an immigration consultation agency. The officer who had attended to him twelve years back, when he first visited this agency, sits across him today as well. Vishal hands in his details and mentions his earlier application. The officer is somewhat surprised to find a man his age wishing to go to Canada to find a job. He looks up Vishal's application history – he had appeared for the necessary exams, got a good score, fulfilled all formalities, submitted the visa fee, and even had a job offer! Surprised, the officer asks Vishal what had happened in the last twelve years.

Vishal, with a choked voice, begins his story.

I was twenty-two when I first applied for the Canadian visa. My father was an electrician who went from home to home, office to office, to repair small and big electric faults. All his life he could not save enough to open a humble electrical goods shop of his own. I had two younger sisters of marriageable age and wished to marry them into well-to-do families. I also wanted my father to have a shop of his own to reduce his travels for petty amounts. But it was not possible to fulfil these dreams being in India. So, I had decided to go to Canada.

My father had been a devotee of a local goddess all his life, visiting her temple and praying since childhood in good times and bad. Most of his life he faced struggles and hardships. But the worst was yet to come.

I worked hard to prepare for my IELTS exams and even applied for a job in Canada. Because my English was not that good, I had to score a decent IELTS band. Everything was moving smoothly. A couple of days before the result, my father told me that he was going to visit the temple the next day to pray for me. It was an auspicious day where the goddess fulfilled the wishes of her devotees who prayed with all their heart standing on their left leg. It seems that I was the result of my parents' prayers offered to the same goddess. I was a little uncomfortable and told him that now that the exams were over nothing could be done. But his belief was unshakable. I did not argue further.

My father left the following morning. Thousands had thronged the temple that day. Many stood in long queues since the wee hours patiently awaiting their turn. It is ironic how the same people cannot wait for ration, railway or bus tickets, or to pay bills at kiosks. I left for the town to deposit the fee and finalize my file for immigration. The following morning, while returning home, I called up my father to inform about the proceedings, but his mobile was switched off. This had never happened before – his work solely depended on phone calls. I tried several times and soon started to worry.

On reaching the bus stand, I received news of a stampede at the goddess's temple, leaving a great many injured or dead. I headed straight to the government hospital where the injured and casualties were taken. Fearing the worst, I went to mortuary and started checking all those who lay dead. I saw many familiar faces, now dead, but was relieved to not find my father's among them.

Just then I received a call from my mother. My father was badly injured and admitted to a private hospital. Both his legs were crushed under the weight of the big iron gate of the temple, which had fallen on the devotees while they tried to escape by climbing over the closed gates. I tried to inquire how the stampede started but received mixed responses. Some said that the *devi* had appeared outside the temple wall, some informed that a heavy-duty wire had fallen on the ground, others related that the roof had collapsed.

Nothing was confirmed.

I reached the hospital. The butcher-surgeon asked me to immediately deposit a lakh to save my father's legs. I had no money. Everything was already paid for my dream escape. Left with no choice my mother sold all her jewellery. Only one of his legs could be saved, the other had to be amputated.

With no bread earner at home, I had to let go of my dreams. I took up my father's profession and wandered from home to home, office to office, repairing small and big electric faults. The income was just about sufficient for the household. I even managed to get my sisters married into good families within our social standing.

Oh! In all this I forgot to tell you that with the blessings of our ancestral goddess, I got a Band 8 in my IELTS exams, and my father was satisfied that his prayers were answered.

As per the wishes of the goddess, my father is still standing on *one leg*.

Questions

Do we really need to gather at and outnumber the capacity of places of worship for our prayers to be heard?

If god is omnipresent, why can't our wishes be fulfilled from our own homes instead?

Do you find yourself questioning such matters based on irrational thinking?

18
56 OFFERINGS

Parth Sharma lives in a posh area in Mumbai. Today he is a successful businessman who has made his own destiny from a humble background. He is a devout follower of Lord Ganesha and owes his thriving business and everything that he has achieved in life to the blessings of Ganesha and his visits to a temple seven kilometres from his home, which he visits routinely every Sunday.

Today he is a happy man. One of his mega business deals has found success. Also because a marriage proposal of his choice for his son has been met with approval – the girl belongs to a rich and renowned family in Mumbai. This was perhaps because of his votive offerings and havan (ritual) done in that temple on the advice of their family priest. He is delighted that his wishes have been fulfilled and to thank the lord he decides to prepare a special treat of *chappan bhog* (56 offerings) for the god the following day, a Sunday. Incidentally, it is also Ganesha Chaturthi, an important festival and auspicious day for the lord's devotees.

On the day of the festival, Parth reaches the temple with his wife Sulekha and buys the required ingredients for the chappan bhog from a famous *halwai* (sweet maker) situated outside the temple, specially prepared in pure desi ghee and as per Hindu purity norms. While Parth and Sulekha carry the two big *thaalis* (big plates) and walk towards the temple, they see a lot of beggars lined outside asking for money or food. Turning a deaf ear, they both walk towards their destination – Lord Ganesha's idol inside the temple. While climbing the stairs they see four long queues of devotees, two for men and the other two for women. The temple is unusually crowded because it is a special occasion. Parth and Sulekha stand in separate queues holding their big thaalis, waiting for their turn. Several hours pass by, but they are still far from the sanctum. The queues are moving slow because all devotees have long prayers to chant, tall demands to make, and big offerings to present.

While waiting, Parth receives a call from home. His servant informs him that some rich, influential relatives of his have come over to invite him to a wedding. Parth instructs him to make the guests comfortable till he reaches back. *This will take a while, and offering the feast will take even longer*, he thinks to himself. To speed things up, he requests the devotees queued up ahead to allow him and his wife to move ahead, but nobody agrees.

Uncomfortable about keeping his guests waiting back home, he decides to return and offer prayers and the feast the following Sunday. As they walk towards the parking lot, a devotee stops them and asks why they are returning without offering prayers. Parth hastily tells him that they are getting late and will come again next week. Without losing an opportunity, the man asks Parth if he will sell him his chappan bhog, for which he was ready to pay more than what Parth had paid. Due to the large crowd, there was a shortage of chappan bhog at the halwai, and this man could not get his. Parth happily agrees as otherwise it would have gone waste. He immediately sells both the thaalis and rushes to his car.

While returning Parth and Sulekha see the same beggars; almost no one was giving them anything. One of them begs Parth for money, '*Agar tumhare bhagwan ka pet bhar gaya ho toh humein bhi kuchh de do.*' (If your god has had his fill, please give us something to eat.) But they ignore and sit in their car and head home. En route, the car stops at a signal and they see a few young children, some without clothes, others injured, and some even crying, running from car to car begging for money or food. As soon as a small girl comes to ask for money towards Parth's car, the signal turns green and they move ahead. Parth is touched by the girl's condition.

After some time they stop at a traffic-heavy crossing. A frustrated old woman knocks hard at their window. Parth takes out some money from his pocket to give her. Parth, who is quite moved by now, asks the driver to park the car on a side, and tells Sulekha to call up the servants back home and apologize for their absence on their behalf.

Parth gets out of the car and goes after the old woman. He asks her to show where she lives, to which she motions him to follow. The wide road has high buildings on both sides. As they walk a little further, the roads become narrower and dirtier. The open sewerage, the dogs, the heaps of garbage, and small houses piled on each other appear next. Parth had never seen the interior of his city. The sight was disturbing: small children playing with mud, sticks, utensils, and even dirty dogs, while their parents were away to work for the rich; old and sick people lying uncared for in their shanties; hunger clearly visible. It was a heart-rending sight. They reach the old woman's house. It is a small room, the entrance of which is so low that one has to bend in order to enter. The so-called kitchen, that is just a shelf on which some utensils and a stove are placed, is inside that room itself, and an old man is lying down on his side. Two small children are sitting beside the old man, one of them is weeping. The old woman tells Parth that her husband has been bedridden since a month and she has lost her son and daughter-in-law in a bus accident. The two children are her grandchildren. She weeps and tells Parth that she needs food for them and herself to stay strong for them. Parth is shaken and distressed. He empties his pockets – his own money as well as what he has received after selling his chappan bhog – and gives it all to the old woman. He tells her to use it for herself and distribute some to her needy neighbours. He assures her that he will visit her every Sunday and help her and the others in this colony.

With a heavy heart Parth returns to the car where Sulekha is waiting. She seems worried because he had taken a long time to return. He tells his wife that from now onwards, as per his routine, he will be visiting this place every Sunday instead of the temple. The chappan bhog will be offered not to god, but to the children of god.

Questions

Do you feel that our god enjoys the meals and offerings in spite of seeing so many people devoid of the basic necessities of life?

Do you think that instead of offering our money and material things to god, we should help instead the children of god?

19

WHEN GOD SPOKE

In a big village lives a very rich man, addressed as 'Seth'. He has two teenaged children – Karan aged sixteen and Natasha, fourteen. He is a firm believer of Lord Shiva. He owns a large farmhouse on the outskirts of the village, not far from his house. It is here that he has erected a big temple, especially for himself, to perform religious *vidhi*s (procedures) and havans, and has installed a huge *murti* (idol) of the lord, which has drawn much attention of the villagers. Even though he has a lot of money, he nurtures an insatiable thirst for more. He does not spare even the poor. He lends them money on interest, keeping their properties or assets as a guarantee, which they are mostly unable to pay back and their assets become his. His wealth is increasing day-by-day, and with this, his greed.

Karan, his son, is a boy with a mind of his own, just opposite of his father. He loves his sister and often bunks school to play with her in their farmhouse, something Seth is unaware of. He feels hurt at his father's actions, but does not dare speak against him.

One day, Seth brings a battery-powered mike for his children from the city. This makes Karan and Natasha excited. But because the noise disturbs their old Dadi,[3] they are prohibited to use it. That same night the children plan to bunk school the next day and go to the farmhouse to play with their new toy. In the morning, they get ready for school as usual, but instead go to the farmhouse. They sing a great many songs and even play hide and seek, using the mike to seek each other. Suddenly they hear the sound of the main gate opening. They are surprised and scared to see their father entering the driveway in his car. If Seth came to know his children had bunked school, they would be scolded and forbidden to enter the farmhouse ever again. It strikes them to hide in the temple, behind the huge Shiva murti.

Seth proceeds towards the idol with the puja thaali in his hands. Failing to pay back the borrowed money with interest, he has grabbed the property of Kaalu, a poor villager. It is verdict day for this case and he has come to pray for its result. Seth stands in front of the murti and starts praying. Both the children know their father well, that he is praying for someone else's doom, and are unhappy.

Suddenly, Karan comes up with an idea. From behind the murti he speaks on the mike: '*Tu ab yahan kya lene aaya hai? Maine pehle hi tujhe bahut kuchh diya hai aur ab tu imaan ki kamaai chhod ke garibon ko beghar karne pe utar aaya hai.'* (What have you come here for now? I have already given you a lot, and now you are looting the poor to profit for yourself?)

Seth is shocked to hear god speak: '*Kya yeh tum ho, prabhu?*' (Is that you, Lord?)

Karan replies: '*Moorakh! Tees saalon se meri puja kar raha hai aur phir bhi shak kar raha hai? Parvati, tum hi baat karo is agyaani moorakh praani se.*' (Fool! You're doubting me after worshipping me for thirty years? Parvati, you speak to this fool.)

Natasha now takes over: '*Agar Shiv krodhit ho gaye to jo bhi tujhe aur tere pitaji ko diya hai, kshan bhar*[4] *mein vaapis le lenge.*' (If Shiva gets angry, he will snatch everything he has given you and your father in a moment.)

Karan wants to get rid of his father, fearing to get caught. He speaks again: '*Bhaag ja yahaan se. Main Hindustan ke sattar crore garibon ki sunoo ya tere jaise laalchi, paapi praaniyon ki?*' (Get lost. Should I listen to the seventy crore poor people of the country or greedy men like you?)

Seth is terrified, begs for mercy, apologizes for his greed, and says: '*Prabhu, maine tees saal aapko bhog lagaya hai, aapka mandir banvaya hai, aur aapko keemti zevar chadaaye hain, phir mujhse kya galti hui jo aap mujhse hi krodhit ho gaye? Main aapko dobaara kaise prasann karun?*' (Lord, I have made offerings to you for the past thirty years, made this temple for you, and even decorated you with expensive jewellery. Where have I gone wrong that you are so angry with me? How do I please you once again?)

Natasha takes over again: '*Agyaani manushya! Bhagwan teri cheezon se khush nahin hote kyunki ye sansaar aur iski vastuen unhon ne hi banaai hain, aur tujhe diya hai taaki tu usko hamaare gareeb bachchon mein baant sake, tere akele ke liye nahin.*' (You brainless human! The Lord doesn't get pleased with your offerings because He has created this worth and its things, and given you these, so that you can distribute these among our poor, not for your consumption alone.)

Seth confronts: '*Bhagwan, mere pitaji ne bahut mehnat se yeh daulat kamai hai. Maine unse bhi zyaada mehnat kari aur unse bhi zyaada kamaaya. Aur aap aadesh de rahe hain ki main isko garibon mein baant dun? Yeh naainsafi ha, Prabhu!*' (Lord, my father worked very hard to amass this wealth. I have worked harder than him and have earned more than him. And you are ordering me to distribute this wealth among the poor? This is unfair, Lord!)

Karan furthers: '*Tere pitaji kya apni kamaai daulat saath le ja sake? Tu bhi nahin le ja paayega.*' (Could your father take his wealth with him? You too won't be able to take it all when you die.)

Seth replies: '*Unhone mujhe di aur main apne bachchon ko doonga.*' (He passed it on to me and I will pass it on to my children.)

Karan then speaks: '*Koi fayda nahin. Woh sab garibon mein baant denge aur unhe swarg mil jayega, woh bhi tere aur tere baap ke paison se, aur tu jalega narak ki aag mein.*' (That won't be of any use. They will distribute your wealth and your father's among the poor and go to heaven, and you will burn in hell's fire.)

Seth worries: '*Nahin, Prabhu, aisa nahin hoga. Mere bachche meri daulat ko is tarah barbaad nahin kar sakte.*' (No, Lord, this won't happen. My children can never waste my wealth this way.)

Karan speaks, angrily: '*Bhagwan tu hai ya main? Bhavishya main dekh sakta hun, tu nahin. Tere bhavishya main abhi badal ke maut likh sakta hun, par thodi amendment karni padedgi.*' (Who is the Lord? I have the power to see the future, not you. I can change your destiny right now and grant you death, but need to make a few amendments first.)

Seth is really frightened now: '*Maafi, Prabhu, maafi! Mujhe marna nahin hai. Main sab achcha karunga. Aap aadesh dijiye.*' (I apologize, Lord! I don't want to die. I will do everything good. Please order.)

Karan orders: '*Kaalu ka ghar vaapis kar aur usse jo byaaj liya hai who bhi.*' (Return Kaalu's house at once and the interest out of the mortgage you have taken.)

'*Bas itna hi? Phir main bach jaaonga?*' (Is that it? I will be saved with this?)

'*Apna ghar, apni dukaan, aur bees laakh ...*' (Your house, your shop, and twenty lakh rupees ...)

Seth, flustered, cuts him short: '*Nahin, Prabhu, yeh main nahin dunga. Chahe aap meri jaan le lijiye.*' (No, Lord, I won't part with these even if you take my life.)

Karan, angrily: '*Moorakh! Pehle poori baat sun le! Yeh cheezein rakh le aur baaki sab kuchch bech ke ek free charitable*

TB hospital banwaa. Tere ilaake mein TB bahut failti hai.' (Fool! First listen to the whole thing. Keep these with you and sell the rest, and with that money build a free charitable TB hospital. There are many who suffer from TB in your area.)

Seth, heavy-heartedly: '*Theek hai, Prabhu. Ab main jaaon?*' (Yes, Lord. May I leave now?)

Karan: '*Haan, dafaa ho ja aur yaad rakh, hospital mein mandir mat banwana. Pehle hi is desh mein mandir, masjid, aur church zyaada hain par school aur hospital kam hain.*' (Yes, get lost! And remember to not erect a temple in the hospital. This country has more of religious places than hospitals.)

Seth agrees, bows, and leaves with a sigh of relief.

Sometimes, the innocence and purity of a child makes him a better human being than the so-called 'experienced' adults claim to be.

Question

Do humans obsess over the creator so much that they forget they are exploiting his creation?

20
PREDICTION

Rajat, a smart, intelligent, practical, twenty-six-year-old boy, is relaxing in his room with a book by Stephen Hawking. It is a Sunday and the week has been hectic at work. The doorbell rings; it is 9 in the morning. Soon he hears his parents speak to someone in the drawing room, which is just next to his room. He realizes it is Babaji.

Rajat is already irritated by his frequent visits. Each time he makes his parents believe in some superstition or the other, or tells them to perform some havan, or ask for donations, to which his parents readily agree. They firmly and blindly believe in him and his predictions. Rajat gets annoyed when he overhears their conversation. Babaji is informing his listeners what is going to happen in the next few months. Agitated, he gets up from his bed, keeps his wallet in his pocket, and goes out of his room, right into the drawing room where the three of them are engrossed in finding out about the future happenings.

Rajat interrupts saying he needs to clarify a query with Babaji. His parents are surprised that their son has finally felt the need to seek Babaji's guidance. His pleased father says that he knew one day his son would come on the right path and believe in the age-old systems of performing vidhis for a better future. Today, he feels that the day has finally come. Leaving their questions aside, his father asks Babaji to attend to his son first.

Rajat asks if Babaji can foretell what is going to happen in the next few minutes, to which the priest nods in agreement. He assures Rajat that he will answer all his questions and give accurate solutions. Rajat enquires him his fee. 'A *dakshina* (fee) of five-hundred-and-one rupees for the first-timers.' Rajat mockingly murmurs, '*Doosri baar zaroorat nahin padegi.*' (A second time won't be necessary.)

He takes out a crisp five-hundred-rupee note from his wallet, keeps a one-rupee coin on top of it, and slides it under his knee. He devotedly folds his hands and asks: '*Kripya batayein, mein aapse pehle sawaal poochhunga ya pehle aapko thappad maarunga?*' (Please tell me, will I ask you a question first or slap you?)

Everyone is stunned. Rajat's father requests Babaji to relax, saying his son is just joking, that it is his nature to be naughty and funny. Babaji is enraged, but somehow controls himself and proceeds: '*Ladka thappad hi maarega, kyunki hum pehle bhi aise bhrasht buddhi logon se mil chuke hain.*' (The boy will first slap, because I have met people with such humour before.)

Rajat's mother is somewhat upset to hear such a verdict about his son and asks Babaji: '*Magar aapne to bhavishyavani ki thi ke humara beta bahut aagyakari aur humare nakshe kadam pe chalne wala niklega, aur iske liye aapne saat din ki puja bhi karwai thi.*' (But you had predicted that our son will be obedient and will follow our footsteps, and for this you had made us perform a seven-day-long puja.)

Babaji covers up: '*Zaroor tumne puja ke samay dhyan nahin lagaya hoga ya tumhara dhyan bhatak gaya hoga. Isliye yeh sab hua hai.*' (I'm sure you were not concentrating during the puja. This is the reason why all this is happening.)

His mother silently agrees: '*Ji, Babaji, dhyan to tikta hi nahin.*' (That is true, Babaji.)

Hearing this, the priest regains his confidence.

Rajat interrupts: '*Mere sawaal ka jawaab nahin dia, Babaji?*' (You didn't answer me, Babaji.)

His father breaks in: '*Babaji, mujhe pata hai, Rajat bahut sanskari hai. Aur yeh sawaal hi poochhega, thappad nahin maarega.*' (Babaji, I know that Rajat is full of values and will only question, not actually slap you.)

Rajat says to father: 'I am serious.'

Babaji: '*Yeh thappad hi maarega.*' (He will slap.)

Father: '*Main guarantee leta hun.*' (I can guarantee he won't.)

Rajat: '*Meri koi guarantee nahin hai.*' (No one can vouch for my actions.)

Finally, Babaji, with his eyes on the money underneath Rajat's knee, says: '*Theek hai, Bachcha, poochho apna sawaal.*' (Alright, Child, ask your question.)

Rajat: '*Poochha to tha, sawaal ab bhi wohi hai.*' (The question remains the same as before.)

A loud slap can be heard.

Question

Do you really believe that there is a way to foretell the future?

If we could predict the future, could we not have prevented many mishaps?

21

THE SMALL MAN

This is a story about two men with two common things: name and job.

The IT firm in Mumbai, where both Sandeep Kumar(s) work at the same position, comprises around fifty staff members. One Sandeep Kumar is a dwarf, addressed as 'Junior', who is humble, intelligent, and good-hearted, always ready to help others. The other is the arrogant, narrow-minded Sandeep Kumar, called by his full name. This Sandeep Kumar is jealous of Junior and often makes fun of his height by calling him 'Chhota Aadmi' (small man) behind his back, which Junior overhears or hears from his colleagues sometimes, but chooses to ignore. At times Sandeep Kumar calls him this right on his face, in the company of his five or six friends who share the same narrow mentality.

The promotion of both Sandeep(s) is due. In the middle of the year a special promotion is announced – a three-bedroom flat with other benefits. Sandeep Kumar demands;

he has a sick mother at home, lying in coma and in need of a separate room. If he does not get this promotion, he has to wait another two years for the next cycle. But he is also aware that his performance has not been satisfactory, and is thus doubtful of this promotion.

The day comes when the promotions will be announced. The CEO takes the name of Sandeep Kumar. Which Sandeep Kumar – Sandeep Junior or Sandeep Kumar – everyone wonders. Sensing this, the CEO says there should be no confusion because everyone knows who has performed well in the past two years. Full of jealousy, a jealous Sandeep Kumar whispers to his friends that this Chhota Aadmi is the CEO's favourite and hence has been promoted.

But the next announcement leaves everyone shocked. The CEO announces that Junior had submitted a written request that if he gets promoted, he would like to pass it on, along with the added benefits, to Sandeep Kumar. Because of his seniority, Sandeep Kumar is eligible for the next promotion, for which Junior can wait another two years. In his request he had also stated that since he is a *chhota sa aadmi* (short/small man), he does not require a bigger house at present, and will wait for his *chhoti si insaan* (short/small woman), which he hopes will surely happen.

Sandeep Kumar is embarrassed. His guilt and shame are clearly visible on his face. He is moved to tears.

Questions

Who is the small man in this story and why?

Are we, in some way, small ourselves? If yes, how do we become large-hearted?

Why are dwarfs differentiated when they have the same brains like us?

They are normal human beings, but are forced to live a different life because of our mindset towards their physical condition which is beyond their control.

22
DINNER DATE

Aryan is an innocent, twenty-seven-year-old bachelor, well settled in a posh colony of Delhi. He is an introvert and has just two friends, Piyush and Ria. Piyush is a smart, outgoing boy and has many friends, but is very close to Aryan because of his simplicity and truthfulness, and over the years they have become best friends. As for Ria, earlier she was just a friend, but now Aryan feels for her differently and wants to marry her.

It is Aryan's birthday today. He thinks it is the perfect occasion to express his feelings for Ria. He plans to take her out for a meal at a fine-dining restaurant in a five-star hotel. He has planned a dinner of French wine, caviar, and lobsters and a specially decorated table. The estimated cost of this dinner would be around thirty thousand rupees, but Ria likes expensive gifts and lavish parties. He is ready to spend this to make the night memorable.

Aryan is very excited. He knows that Ria will appreciate his way of expressing his love for her. En route the restaurant

Piyush calls to wish him. He thanks him and excitedly tells him the plan for the evening. Piyush is surprised and cross-checks if it is the same Ria. Ria Mahajan, their classmate from college. When Aryan confirms it is indeed the same Ria, Piyush asks him to stop the car and listen to him carefully. He tells him that Ria is a fraud and has been fooling boys like him for expensive gifts and to get pampered. Piyush also discloses that the two of them were together the previous night in a hotel room and he had made voice and video recordings to prove that she was cheating on him. He sends these to Aryan and asks him to decide for himself if he still wants to continue with his plan.

Aryan is shocked to hear and see the recordings of similar conversations she was having with Piyush. Numb, he does not know what to do next. He sees an NGO-run shelter home for the poor next to where he had stopped his car. Shattered and disappointed, he goes inside and donates the thirty thousand rupees, which he had saved for the date. The head of the home assures him he would receive a receipt for the donation, as per standard procedure.

For the first two nights Aryan gets no sleep. But soon he begins to counsel himself and now starts to feel better. Things gradually start to fall back to the usual routine. The fifth morning he receives a receipt from the shelter home along with a note of thanks and the details of how his money was spent. In the note they have explained that there were a total of 157 homeless people residing there, whose per person meal for a day was Rs 60. With his donation, they had bought 500 meals for all residents. He is shocked to learn that his one dinner served so many hungry and needy people.

Aryan feels immensely happy. He immediately picks up his mobile phone and types out a message to all his contacts requesting them to donate money or household items and clothes on their birthdays or otherwise. He ends with a personal guarantee that there is no better feeling than what one experiences after this noble deed.

Questions

Have you ever thought of the starving people and their hunger?

Would you help such needy people?

According to recent FAO estimates, 194.4 million people are undernourished in India in 2019. That is 14% of the population of the country.

23
JAUNDICE

Saurabh is a full-time, middle-class businessman, but takes time out to volunteer as a social reformer and an activist. He is a rationalist, and is witty and has a sharp presence of mind. He researches and writes about the superstitions and misconceptions prevalent in the Indian society. For this he interviews many babas (godmen) and yogis. Writing, for him, was once a hobby, but now it is more of a moral and social responsibility – for the welfare of the society, thus doing his bit for the country.

His best friend, Ramesh, comes from a rich and influential family. His family has good connections in society, especially with politicians and those from the high class. His wife, Neeta, and his parents are strong followers of Dera Kasht Haran, an organization run by a baba. This baba is forty-five, six-feet tall, well built, and wealthy, who owns many luxury cars and big bungalows. He has a strong following who visit to his dera regularly.

Ramesh has been suffering from jaundice for the last fifteen days. No medication is helping his condition. He has not been eating properly, and now his immunity has deteriorated. Saurabh has visited Ramesh at the hospital and is really worried for him. On his third day of hospitalization, Ramesh lost consciousness. The jaundice has affected his liver and other vital organs. The doctors cannot say why medication is not working on him and are not confident about saving his life.

Ramesh's mother-in-law suggests they seek Babaji's blessings. In the past they have witnessed many miracles. They have seen people coming with generous gifts to thank Babaji for his *mehar* (blessings). So, Neeta and Ramesh's mother reach the dera to meet Babaji. They sit before him with folded hands and wet eyes, narrating the worsening condition of Ramesh. Babaji closes his eyes and concentrates for some time and then assures them that they need not worry because Ramesh would get better. He advises them to get a specially designed puja, havan and some other rituals done. Some pundits from Babaji's dera reach Ramesh's home and arrange the havan immediately. The family spends a lot of money on these rituals because they believe Ramesh will heal as a result.

On the fifth day of the havan, Ramesh is declared out of danger. He returns home after eight days and soon recovers fully. His family is indebted to Babaji, and invite him and his chelas (disciples) home for a lavish lunch the following Sunday. They even keep aside a donation of fifty-one thousand rupees for Babaji.

On Sunday, Babaji arrives with his team. Saurabh and his wife, unaware of the gathering, reach Ramesh's home to meet him. On seeing the fleet of luxury cars parked he assumes some politicians must have come to wish Ramesh good health, but is surprised to see Babaji and his retinue. Saurabh had written some articles against the superstitions of this baba. The tall, well-built Babaji is seated on a special, huge, silver chair, thronged by numerous chelas in yellow robes. Ramesh and his wife are sitting dedicatedly with folded hands in front of Babaji, listening to his *pravachans*.[5]

Saurabh greets his friend's father, who, well aware of his beliefs, takes him deliberately to Babaji to seek his blessings. Saurabh obeys out of respect. But he does not bow his head. Babaji realizes this person has been brought to him without his will, without any devotion. He is made to sit next to his friend, and his wife, beside Ramesh's wife.

Within a few minutes lunch is announced. All the chelas and other people go outside to the garden where the lunch has been laid out. A special arrangement is made for Babaji in the lobby. A big bowl of warm water infused with rose petals is brought to him to clean his hands. Then arrives a big thaali with various kinds of dishes, specially made by Neeta in shudh desi ghee. Babaji starts his lunch, and Ramesh's family and his in-laws, with folded hands, are happy to see him relishing his meal. Ramesh has not allowed him to leave without having lunch. Saurabh watches all this quietly yet uncomfortably, something he has written against numerous times.

A platter of different kinds of sweets arrives for Babaji. As he is about to pick a piece of barfi, a *sadhvi* (female disciple), who was standing right behind him, stops him from eating it. Babaji is a diabetic and his sugar levels have been on a rise for the past two weeks. Babaji obeys her, as if he usually follows what is suggested by this sadhvi. Once he is finished, a bowl with rose water is brought to him to wash his hands.

Saurabh has been watching the series of events unfold with great curiosity. He now stands up and bows before Babaji as if to seek his blessings. Babaji is happy thinking he has converted another non-believer, but what Saurabh asks next makes him believe he is nothing but a threat to his empire.

Saurabh politely asks him if he could cure fatal diseases like cancer and save his friend from deathbed, why could he not cure his own diabetes? Babaji looks angrily towards Ramesh's mother-in-law who had invited him for lunch and is now made to face such an uncomfortable question. She feels embarrassed for not being able to help him in this awkward situation. But Babaji is clever, and says since he is a messenger of god he has the power to cure others by taking it upon his own body.

Saurabh knew Babaji would cook up an appropriate answer. He is ready for the second attack – he asks Babaji to cure Ramesh's father's hypothyroidism, an autoimmune disease, and blood pressure. Babaji is stunned. Saurabh knows that Babaji's own daughter is suffering from systemic lupus erythematosus, an autoimmune disease, and had been on medication, even steroids, for many years. She was hospitalized the previous year for fifteen days when specialists had been called from London to cure her. He asks Babaji that he should have at least cured his daughter. Sensing Babaji's discomfort, the same sadhvi intervenes saying it is time for his weekly satsang (spiritual gathering), and that he should visit him at his dera to seek clarifications.

Babaji leaves in a haste, leaving those present puzzled. Saurabh giggles, mockingly.

Ramesh is angry with his friend. His mother-in-law leaves with Babaji and asks him to drop Neeta home because she does not want her daughter to be in the presence of someone who has insulted Babaji.

Saurabh leaves quietly, thinking he was present in the wrong place at the wrong time. Perhaps the same thought crossed Babaji's mind too.

Questions

Do you think that many of us have lost their basic common sense of evaluating facts because of some misleading babas, who have convinced people to live in a fool's paradise?

Do you think that there should be a chapter on logical and rational thinking in school curriculum to help future generations distinguish between fact and myth?

24
PROPERTY

Bishamber Nath is a rich Marwadi who has worked hard all his life to become the wealthy man that he is today. Both he and his wife are pure vegetarians, religious, and follow rituals devoutly. He is sitting in the lobby of his house with his wife Shakuntala and a lawyer friend to give *paargati* (disown and disinherit) to his only son Som Nath, who has crossed all his limits and cannot be controlled anymore. Both Bishamber Nath and Shakuntala are grief-stricken, but they have to take this extreme step and disown him from family wealth.

Being the only child, Somi, as he is lovingly called, was pampered since childhood. When either of his parents scolded him for wrongdoing, the other shielded him. Som Nath has grown to be someone without any respect for his parents or relatives, spoilt, arrogant, alcoholic, and even a womanizer. He even does not like his name because to him it seems old-fashioned. Till the age of eighteen, his parents fulfilled all his demands thinking it is just a phase and he will grow out of it with age.

Somi is about twenty-four now, and his lifestyle and habits are getting worse. He sleeps till late in the afternoon, then gets ready and leaves to party, only to return late in the night, that too completely drunk. Every night Shakuntala stays awake out of worry till her son returns.

Bishamber Nath was made aware of his son's habits. He got to know that, apart from smoking and drinking, and then getting into fights, he visits prostitutes, and even has a keep, a bar dancer, on whom he spends a great amount. Being a housewife and staying at home all day, Shakuntala was unaware of her son's whereabouts. Despite Bishamber Nath's repeated efforts to tell Shakuntala that all was lost, she had been hopeful that her son will change one day. The love for her son was too great until one night.

That night Somi crossed all his limits. He reached home late at night, completely drunk, with a prostitute by his side, who was supporting him on her shoulder. Furious, Shakuntala did not allow Somi inside the house. That night she took a stand to agree with her husband's decision to cut him off the family wealth and donate everything they had to a charitable trust after their death.

This is why the lawyer, a good friend of Bishamber Nath, is present in their home today. He has brought all legal documents of disownment along with their will. The lawyer explains and convinces Bishamber and Shakuntala to reconsider their decision, warning that they might lose their only son as a result of this harsh decision. But they are adamant; they have already lost their son, who, at present, does not bother to even look at their faces. Heartbroken, they both sign the papers.

When Somi wakes up in the afternoon, he is surprised to see the lawyer. The lawyer informs him of his parents' decision. Somi screams in anger and leaves the house threatening to never return. Both the parents are disturbed, but what had to be done has now been done.

Within three days Somi returns. Bishamber and Shakuntala are having their tea when the doorbell rings. The servant informs them that Somi is standing at the door and is in a bad condition. He falls at his parents' feet apologizing and begging for one chance to prove that he has learnt a lesson. He promises he will mend his ways and live in the house according to their likes. Shakuntala, who was already broken, gestures to Bishamber to give their son a second chance. Seeing his wife's condition and the way Somi has been begging for forgiveness, he agrees reluctantly.

Since that day, Somi is a totally changed person. He wakes up early, takes a bath, and participates in the morning pooja and has become a religious person. He has also started working with his father and has quit drinking and smoking. He makes an extra effort to treat his parents well.

But his intentions are not quite noble. During the three days he was not at home, when no one was willing to give him refuge, the insult he faced and his greed for wealth made Somi devise a plan: to get back to his parents. The good-son act was only to fool his parents and regain their trust. In the early days, Bishamber was suspicious, but was soon convinced by his son's changed behaviour. Three months have passed and the family is happy, especially the parents. Bishamber called his lawyer and made Somi their legal heir once again.

One day, Somi asks his parents about the pilgrimage they wanted to take with their son. While earlier he could not understand, he believes he should fulfil this desire now. He would also pray to god for forgiveness for all the sins he had committed in the past. His parents are overjoyed and decide to leave the very next day around noon. He plans a visit to three temples out of which one was on the way to a big shrine located on the banks of the Ganga. He shows keenness to visit this temple particularly because it is known as a place where pilgrims seek forgiveness. Throughout the journey he plays sacred songs in the car to impress his parents. They visit two temples. Because it is winters, it gets dark soon. They reach the river from where they need to board a small wooden boat to reach the temple which is at the distant end of the river. The temple appeared to be very small, but Bishamber and Shakuntala were happy at their son's gesture and did not question his intentions.

Somi asks the boatman to lend his boat: he will row it himself to the temple. He pays the boatman some extra money and says they will return in about three hours. Somi carefully makes his parents sit at one end of the boat, while he stands at the other end to row. Bishamber and Shakuntala are engrossed in conversation. They feel a sudden change in Somi's behaviour, but ignore it.

As they reach the middle of the river, Somi stops rowing. He takes out a sharp axe from his backpack. On asked why he is carrying an axe, Somi says in order to fulfil their wish of meeting god. His parents are shocked. They understand his intent and fear for their lives. They beg him to not kill them. He could keep all property and money. But Somi smiles, saying he does not want their *bheekh*,[2] that it is his right to own all the wealth that they tried to snatch from him. He walks to the middle of the boat and tells them that he will send them to god since they are so eager to meet them. His parents shout for help, but there is no one to rescue them in the middle of the river in the dark. Somi tells his scared parents that he is not stupid to kill them and land behind bars. He demands all insurance claims, as he will prove their death accidental. He starts chopping the boat and soon water starts filling up the boat. He leaves his parents to drown and swims back to the shore.

Three months have passed. Somi is sitting in the lobby at his house drinking with his girlfriend, the same bar dancer, when the doorbell rings. The insurance claims of his deceased parents have arrived, cheques worth a crore! Somi now has control over the property, all bank balance, and the insurance. He promises his girlfriend to buy the dance bar where she worked. He will pay a token amount of fifty lakhs this evening, and the remaining once he encashes the cheques. Both seem overjoyed.

Later that night he heads out for the dance bar. He parks his car on the other side of the road, picks up the bag of money, and walks up to the bar. He has been drinking since evening and he is so drunk that he does not notice the speeding BMW sports car while crossing the road. The driver and his girlfriend, both drunk, do not notice him either. He crashes the car into Somi, and throws him off at a distance. The bag of money escapes and the notes fly in the air. Somi dies on the spot. Both passengers step out, see the scattered money and the bleeding victim. He says, '*Yeh saala koi chor lagta hai jo bank loot kar bhaag raha tha. Pata nahin police inaam degi ya sazaa is accident case mein.*' (Looks like a thief who has robbed a bank. No clue if the police will reward or punish us in this accident case.)

One can hear police siren approaching now.

Question

Why do we try to accumulate wealth through wrong means when we cannot take anything with us when we die?

25
GARBAGE COLLECTOR

Raju is a twenty-two-year-old garbage collector, who collects waste from a high-rise residential building located in a posh colony of Mumbai. All the families residing in the twelve-floored building are good and loving, or at least not rude to him, except for the family living on the topmost floor. It is occupied by a joint family, jewellers by profession, who have converted four apartments into one big apartment. They own luxury cars, have a lot of money, and lead a lavish lifestyle, but are high-headed and arrogant.

Raju has never misbehaved with anyone, but is always ill-treated by this family. He is not allowed to touch their door, let alone the doorbell. Every day he has to request their personal guard to ring the bell for him to do his job. If in the absence of the guard, he rings the bell, he is insulted and humiliated when they order their servant to clean the doorbell in front of him. Gifts during festivals are handed out by their servants.

One day on climbing to the top floor, Raju suddenly feels dizzy; he had not been feeling well since morning. He sits against the wall of that family's apartment, not knowing what would happen next. The younger daughter-in-law of the house sees him and immediately starts yelling at the kurewala (garbage collector), accusing him of gaining sympathy of others by such fake acts. Raju gulps his insult and with great difficulty goes downstairs in tears. That family always insult him and call him 'kurewala'; never by his name as they do not even know his name.

Mr Gupta, the sixty-year-old secretary of the society, notices his condition and offers him the stool on which he was sitting and brings him a glass of water. Seeing his humble gesture, Raju breaks down. On asking he tells Guptaji of all that he has been suffering at the hands of the family living on the top floor. He requests to be relieved of his duties to collect garbage from that apartment. Guptaji explains that he cannot boycott or leave this work as it was against the rules of the building, which offers these facilities to the residents against a monthly deposit. But at the same time he reassures Raju that he will ensure their behaviour towards the young boy improves. He advises Raju to continue with his job as usual, except collecting garbage from their house for a week.

Lata Aunty, the head of the family on the topmost floor, does not know what to do with the piled-up garbage bags because these have not been collected for two days.

In the evening of the second day, she complains to the secretary, Guptaji. He assures her he will speak with Raju. After some time, he replies to Lata Aunty that Raju had forgotten, but will surely collect the next day. Next day comes and Raju again does not turn up. Guptaji answers the queries of the family saying he is unwell but will attend to it the next day.

For four days new excuses are given and the garbage outside this apartment keeps piling up. Lata Aunty asks her servant to fetch garbage boys from the neighbouring buildings to collect their garbage. But they all refuse because they have divided their work between buildings and will not go against their union rules, not even if they are paid extra money. In the past, Lata Aunty's family always got their problems solved through money or power, but this time both failed. So they hire a separate car, a pick-up van, specially to dispose the garbage bags; their owned cars are too fancy to do menial tasks like this.

On the fifth day they catch hold of Raju, who says his rickshaw is full and cannot take their garbage, and that he will visit their apartment the next day. Seeing the big black bags being carried away in a pick-up van daily, Lata Aunty's neighbour taunts her which leaves her embarrassed: what are they carrying away secretly in the bags daily, shifting their mass wealth in instalments, perhaps?

Being a joint family, their household produces a lot of garbage daily. They all are tired of this and need a permanent solution.

The sixth day too Raju does not turn up. They visit Guptaji and angrily tell him to take action. Guptaji pretends to be angry as well, but soon reverts saying Raju's mobile is switched off and hence cannot be contacted.

On the seventh day too when the garbage is not collected, Lata Aunty along with her husband demand Guptaji to fire Raju. This time Guptaji tells them upfront that Raju is not ready to collect their garbage as it smells foul. He also tells them that he cannot fire him as no other resident has ever complained against him. He has been performing his duty well, he comes daily, on time, is careful to not spill anything. He works dedicatedly all seven days a week, without taking any off, come rain or storm.

Lata Aunty and her husband sense something is wrong and ask Guptaji what the real matter is. Guptaji then tells them that it is their behaviour, which is not acceptable, be it to the little boy or to the building society. He suggests them to tell each family member to behave properly and respect the garbage collector because he is also a human after all. The only difference is that he is not privileged like them solely because of marginalization done by the privileged lot. They have their own daily battles to fight, and the least we can do to ease their lives is to show a little respect.

They both now understand that they were wrong in treating Raju the way they did. They assure Guptaji they will mend their ways.

The next morning, the doorbell rings and Lata Aunty opens the door. Seeing Raju at the door, she says, '*Aa gaya, Beta? Abhi kude ke bags mangwati hoon.*' (You've arrived, Son? Let me get the garbage bags for you.)

She calls out to the maidservant, '*Shanta Bai, kuda laao aur baahar ladke ko paani bhi pilao.*' (Shanta Bai, bring the garbage and get a glass of water for this boy.)

Suddenly, she turns back and asks him, '*Arre, Beta, tumhara naam to poochhna bhool hi gayi. Kya hai tumhara naam?*' (I forgot to ask your name.)

'Raju,' he replies.

She again calls out to the maidservant, '*Abhi tak paani nahin laaye? Raju ko pyaas lagi hogi. Kitni garmi hai aaj subah hi.*' (You haven't brought the water yet? Raju must be thirsty. It's so hot from morning itself today.)

Questions

Do these people, who work tirelessly to make our lives better and comfortable, not deserve respect and better wages to live a dignified life of their own?

How many of us will change our ways and go a step forward to improve their lives?

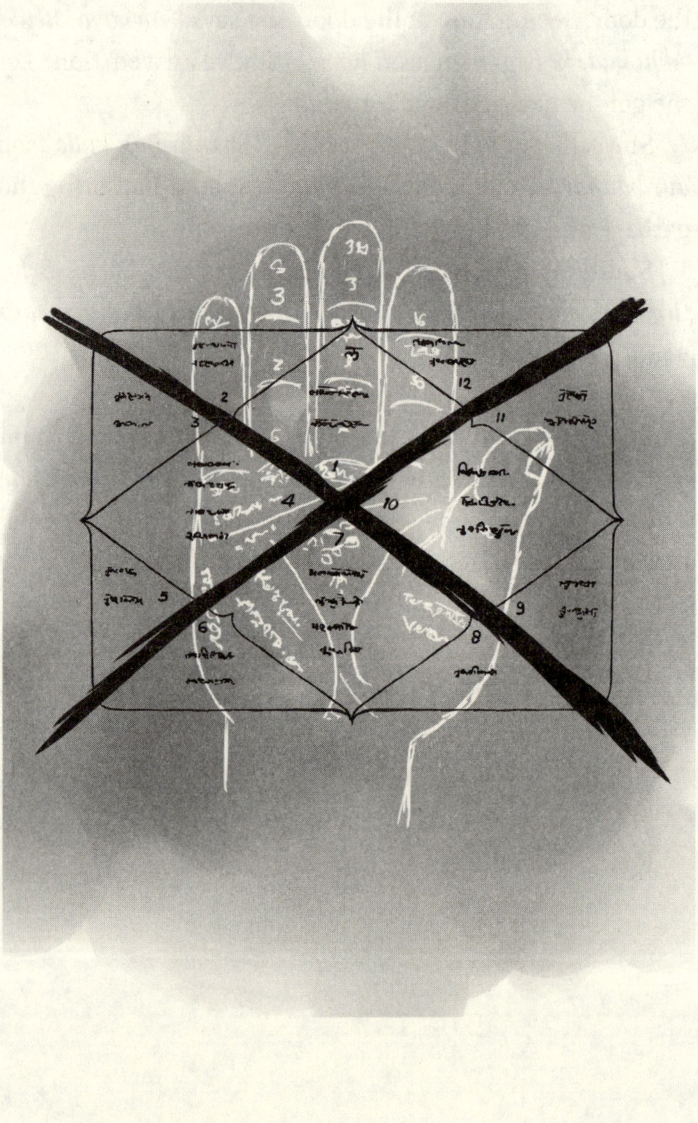

26

HOROSCOPE

Satish and Meeta have three children: two sons, Vishal, twenty-eight, and Rahul, twenty-four, and a daughter, Anamika, eighteen. Meeta is superstitious by nature and Satish follows almost everything his wife asks him to. Their eldest son, Vishal, is divorced and has left India to settle abroad. He had settled for a love marriage, against Meeta's consent. She believes that the real reason for their divorce is because their *kundali*s (horoscopes) were not matched – the bride belonged to a Sikh family and they did not believe in kundalis.

The younger son, Rahul, has now reached marriageable age. Meeta is worried about the fate of Rahul and fears that he too will leave her and go if his marriage does not work out. Meeta does not want to take any chances this time. One of her very close friends suggests a fortune-teller (*jyotshi*), who is believed to be a master in matching kundalis.

Meeta and Satish, along with the girl's parents, visit this Jyotshi, with kundalis of the prospective couple. A young girl of twenty wearing a white saree, the Jyotshi's daughter Sakshi, tells them that he is performing pooja and will attend to them shortly. She makes them comfortable and goes to get tea and snacks. Satish is surprised to see such a young girl in white. The room in which they are sitting seems quite lavish. After about ten minutes, the Jyotshi enters the room and greets them. He seems to be a wealthy man and is wearing a crisp white kurta pyjama and several gold chains and rings. He takes all details and starts calculating the *gun* and *dosh* (good and bad) of both kundalis.

Meanwhile, Sakshi brings them tea and snacks. As she leaves the room, Satish asks out of curiosity, '*Yeh bitiya ne safed saree kyun pehni hai?*' (Why is your daughter dressed in white?)

Jyotshiji replies, '*Daamadji ki pichhle saal accident mein mrityu ho gayi.*' (My son-in-law passed away in an accident last year.)

Both the couples look at and rise, telling Jyotshiji, '*Humein aagya dijiye.*' (Please allow us to leave.)

A surprised Jyotshiji says, '*Magar abhi poori kundaliyan to padhi hi nahin.*' (But I haven't yet gone over the horoscopes.)

They keep walking. '*Arre apni kundaliyan to le jao.*' (Take your horoscopes.)

One of them pauses and answers, '*Ab inki zaroorat nahin hai.*' (There's no need of them anymore.)

Questions

How could a Jyotshi, who did not know his own daughter's future, foretell someone else's?

Are marriages not successful without matching horoscopes?

Can we predict the future of complex human relationships in a marriage which change all the time?

27
DOG AND MAN

Sunita is now fifty-five; she had become a widow at the young age of twenty-five. She has brought up her only son, Aman, all by herself. Her only support system is her best friend, Lata, who lives in the neighbouring building. Lata is a caring and helpful person and has always guided Sunita in all matters. Sunita's main goal has been to secure Aman's future. She has given him a good education to be able to stand on his own feet.

Now that Aman is an independent, grown man, Sunita is relieved of her duties, but feels lonely at home when he goes off for work or on official tours. To keep herself occupied, she adopts a dog, Pluto.

Aman has married his lover, Ria, and they are blessed with a son and a daughter. Though there are some differences between Sunita and Ria, which lead to quarrels at times, Sunita takes very good care of her grandchildren. Whenever she is upset or tensed, either Lata or Pluto help release her stress. Aman now has no time for her because he is busy with his own family. He is growing more distant from his mother each day.

Meanwhile, Aman gets a promotion and decides to move to America with his family. Ria, who does not like Sunita, or Lata, or even Pluto, is happy dreaming of the independent life in America. Aman relocates to America with Ria and the two kids. To cope up with her loneliness, Sunita keeps herself busy with household chores and caring for Pluto.

Six months pass.

Ria's dreams of an independent life turns into a hectic routine. She has to let go of her job because she has to manage all household work and both children all by herself. In desperation, she convinces Aman to call his mother to America for their help.

In all these six months, Aman has hardly ever called his mother, but now given the situation at his home he starts calling her daily. This makes Sunita both surprised and happy, thinking that perhaps distance has revived her son's love for her. Lata, however, is not convinced and tries to warn Sunita of her son's intentions, which to her do not seem noble.

Finally, Aman asks Sunita to move to America. She agrees, but on the condition to bring Pluto along. Aman refuses because his apartment is not pet-friendly; moreover, it is expensive to keep a dog in America. He tells her that they will call for Pluto after some months. After some hesitation and reluctance, Sunita finally agrees. Aman sponsors her travel to America, but not Pluto.

Just five days are left for Sunita to leave for America. She sends Pluto to Lata beforehand so that he can adjust with her. But being so attached to Sunita, he is not able to bear the separation. He does not eat or drink properly and keeps running back home whenever he gets a chance. Sunita is quite worried about him and keeps discussing his condition with Aman almost everyday. He listens patiently for some days, but now this is getting a bit too much for him.

Finally, the day arrives. Sunita locks the house and goes down with her luggage. She sees Lata from a distance, bidding her farewell along with Pluto. Pluto, on seeing Sunita, frees himself and runs towards her. He clasps her legs tightly and whines. Sunita too is very upset and begins to cry. Just then Aman calls his mother to check if she has left for the airport. Sunita is sobbing and starts telling him about Pluto. Hearing the talk about the dog again Aman loses his patience. 'In America, it is different to keep parents and dogs because money has to be spent to keep dogs.' He does not talk about the other aspect that in the US, the government gives pension to its retired citizens.

Sunita is shocked and realizes what Aman is up to. '*Aur parents ko rakne ke paise milte hain?*' (And do you get paid for the upkeep of parents?)

She adds, angrily, '*Aur woh bhonkte bhi nahin aur tumhare bachche paalne ke saath, chup chaap tumhara saara kaam bhi karte hain.*' (Parents don't bark, and along with caring for your children they also silently go about doing all your work.)

Aman is ashamed.

Sunita leaves the bag. She hugs Pluto, picks him up, and starts moving towards her apartment. Lata follows her with her bag.

Questions

How justified is it for young children to leave their parents alone at an age when they need them the most?

How cruel is it to shatter the routines and emotions of old parents for their own selfish purposes?

28
MY FAMILY

Sumesh is a thirty-four-year-old man working in a company as a manager. His wife, Alka, a housewife, is a fashion freak. She is least interested in household chores and is more keen to attend kitty parties and get-togethers. Rahul is their eight-year-old son. Sumesh's sick, bedridden mother also lives with them. She is hard of hearing and has been asking her son for a hearing aid for a long time, which he says he will get her once he receives the bonus. The whole house is run by the servant.

Rahul is very attached to his parents and his grandmother. He keenly observes his parents and tries to follow them as all children do. His parents try to inculcate good manners in him – never lie, respect elders, help the poor, do not abuse others. But he hardly sees them following these tenets.

One day Sumesh comes home from work early and is very happy.

He has been promoted and received a bonus. Alka is not home as usual. He goes to his mother's room where he finds Rahul pressing her legs. Seeing her son, the old mother asks Sumesh of his well-being and to buy her the required hearing aid. Just then Alka enters and Sumesh immediately leaves the room to give her the good news. Rahul follows outside to meet his mother, he has not seen her since he came back from school. He stops at the door because he can hear his parents talk. Sumesh asks Alka to buy a hearing aid for his mother, but she suggests not to waste money on it; one does not know how long she will live anyway.

Instead, Alka demands gold jewellery for herself. Sumesh hands her the money and asks her to deal with the old woman because he cannot answer if she asks for the hearing aid once again. All through the conversation they do not notice Rahul outside. Being a sensitive child, Rahul does not like what he just heard. Disappointed, he goes straight back to his grandmother to press her legs. In some time Alka arrives to tell her mother-in-law that Sumesh had not received his bonus this year, so they would get her the hearing aid either next year or when they have saved some money. Rahul is surprised to hear his mother lie.

Next morning Rahul hears his father asking for a sick leave. He wants to relax the whole day and watch the cricket match from home.

Some days pass. Sumesh receives a call from Rahul's class teacher complaining that he has not been doing his homework saying he is unwell. Sumesh lies to cover up, saying indeed his son is not keeping well. Both parents are angry that their son has lied at school. On reaching home from office, Sumesh scolds Rahul hard, but Rahul tries to explain that his father too lies.

One day Rahul gets an assignment from his school: to write an essay on 'My Family'. Ever since they received the phone call from school, both Sumesh and Alka have been paying attention to the activities of their son. They sit with him and make him write the essay. They narrate to him what he should write: that his father is honest, hard-working, and a man of his words, and his mother is a housewife who takes good care of the house, her child, and her bedridden mother-in-law. But when Rahul finishes writing the essay, he is in a dilemma: what has been narrated is not how things are.

The following day Rahul takes the essay to school. As Rahul walks up to submit it, he pauses. He goes back to his seat and adds a concluding sentence:

I wish all this becomes a reality one day.

Rahul then walks up to the teacher and submits his essay.

Question

How can our children grow up with good ideals and manners if we flout them ourselves?

Are we taking away from a child the possibility of them shaping the future of our country by not acting on what we speak?

29

MY FATHER, MY HERO

The bond of children with their parents is one of love. It is commonly believed that the personality of a child develops from what they learn from their elders, especially parents. Also it is a common belief that while a son is more attached to his mother, a daughter always looks up to her father as her hero.

This is the story of Reena, an eighteen-year-old, elegant and delicate girl, how her hero becomes helpless when he is not able to protect his daughter from the notorious street boys and his close relative due to his weaknesses, and how she in turn helps her hero.

Reena studies in Class 12 and her final examinations are approaching. She walks to her school and back every day since it is quite near her home. Today as she leaves for school, some notorious street boys notice Reena, but she is oblivious to her surroundings. On her way back, the same boys block her way and start to tease her and make obscene gestures. This makes Reena very uncomfortable. She is too timid physically and mentally to confront the notorious lot. She runs back home sweating and completely scared. Looking at her state, her father figures something was wrong. He first offers her water, and then asks caringly what had happened. Now calmed down and feeling secured, Reena narrates the whole incident. She hugs her father tightly and weeps and pleads him to save her from the goons.

Her father is disturbed and agitated and decides to teach the boys a lesson the next morning. He sees them waiting for Reena en route her school. He threatens them with a police complaint. But the boys are shameless and start hurling abuses at him. They beat him up and tear his clothes. Unable to do anything, he goes back home embarrassed. He shuts himself up in the bedroom and weeps silently. After about three or four, he comes out and watches TV in the drawing room, ignoring Reena as he is in no condition to face her. Reena is devastated to see her father like this.

The next few days either her mother or her father accompany Reena to school and back. Once she gets admission in college, a college van picks her up and drops her home regularly. Some months pass by but Reena and her father have still not recovered from the incident. One day Reena goes to her Bua's (aunt) house. Bua is not around, but her husband greets her in their drawing room. Finding Reena all alone, he tries to molest her, but luckily Reena escapes.

She had not even reached back home when her uncle calls up Reena's father accusing her to be character-less. But her father is angry and starts shouting at him in protest. At this point the uncle threatens him to not reveal the incident to his sister or anyone else, lest he will file for a divorce and also defame Reena publically.

Once again Reena's father is helpless. He is so disturbed by these incidents that he goes into depression and even stops going to office.

Reena cannot bear to see her hero getting shattered bit-by-bit each day. She decides to take matters into her own hands. She looks up the Internet on how to protect oneself from sexual predators. She learns self-defence techniques and joins a martial arts academy. Soon, with her dedication, she achieves the black belt. She even opens her own martial arts academy to teach young girls self-defence, an important need for every girl in today's times.

One day a father comes to her academy with his daughter, Meghna. While Meghna wants to join kathak classes, her father insists she joins Reena's academy. He will soon be transferred to a different city and Meghna must live by herself, thus the emphasis on learning self-defence for her own protection.

Witnessing the tiff between the father and daughter, Reena wishes to speak with Meghna alone. She narrates incidents from her own life, how her father and she had suffered because she was not strong enough to fight for herself. She makes the young girl realize that she should become strong so that what had happened to Reena's hero never happens to hers. Meghna is moved and so convinced that she runs out and hugs her father. She agrees to join self-defence classes and assures her father that she will be able to take care of herself while he is in a different city.

Questions

Are self-defence classes more important than dance lessons for our girls these days? Is this because there is not enough security in our cities for women?

Are all parents aware of what is happening with their daughters?

30

NEW WRITER

Rakesh is a handsome man with an impressive personality. He works at a private bank as a manager. His wife Ayesha, is a homemaker. Though her husband is earning satisfactorily, Ayesha longs for a better lifestyle. Rakesh has nurtured a passion for writing since his childhood, which he could not pursue because his parents did not consider it a stable career option.

Now that he is well-settled and his parents have passed away, his passion for writing revives. In his free time, he writes long and short stories. He writes on social issues and thinks Bollywood is the best platform to share his social message with the masses. But being new to this field, he does not know how to get his writings forward. He is so passionate that he is willing to sacrifice his career for this.

He meets Manoj, a PR consultant, to launch him as a screenwriter in Bollywood. Manoj explains how he can introduce Rakesh to various producers and directors, and gives him the idea of getting his stories published as a novel and his articles in newspapers. Rakesh is very excited. But for all this Manoj lays out a budget of fifty lakh rupees. Rakesh is disappointed because he has only around twenty-five lakhs to launch his career, including all savings and the VRS.

Seeing Rakesh's disappointment, Manoj suggests a better idea with his budget, where investment is less and return will be in the form of respect, fame, and a lot of money. He proposes to make him a Famous Baba. But for that he will have to change his story's subject. He tells him that he needs to build a fool's paradise where people are lured in the name of going to heaven after death, get problems concerned with their future solved and offer suggestions on other religious beliefs and disbeliefs. He explains that this way donations will pour in automatically to him.

Rakesh leaves in disbelief. How can he turn his social cause into that of a fake identity? He leaves Manoj's office saying he will surely find some noble soul to help fulfil his dream, that too in his budget.

Ten months pass.

One morning Manoj enters his office and is surprised to find Rakesh waiting for him. He seems depressed and heartbroken. His hair has grown and he has a messy beard. Manoj pretends as if he has not recognized him. Rakesh instantly begins, '*Woh Baba wala package hi de do, par ikkis lakh mein.*' (Give me that Baba package, but for twenty-one lakhs.)

Manoj mockingly asks, '*Kyun bhai, baaki char lakh ka kya hua?*' (Whatever happened to the remaining four lakhs?)

Rakesh replies, '*Woh to pichhle dus mahine mein travelling, hotels, aur aise hi kuchh kharchon mein kharch hogaye. Magar kuchh na hua.*' (That got spent in travelling, hotels, and so on over the last ten months. But nothing came off it.)

Manoj passes a naughty smile and winks at him. '*Ho jaayega. Ab to tum lagte bhi baba hi ho, magar pandrah per cent commission deni hogi kaam chalne pe aur haan is ikkis lakh ka bill nahin milega, kyunki yeh secret project hota hai, saath mein tumhara GST bhi bach jaayega.*' (Don't worry, it'll work now. You even look like a baba now, but I will charge fifteen per cent commission, and you won't receive a receipt for the twenty-one lakhs because this is a secret project and it will help save you some extra bucks because you don't have to pay the GST.)

Questions

Are brokers really needed for your talent to reach its destination? Was it necessary for Manoj to exploit Rakesh and turn him towards a wrong motive?

Is it necessary to change your noble motive into a corrupt one to earn money and fame? Could Rakesh not have continued with his job as a bank manager?

31 NIRVANA

Sachin is a successful businessman of forty-six. His wife, Misha, is forty-four and they have two intelligent sons. Misha takes good care of the family and the house. Sachin has a perfect life anyone can possibly wish for. But he is not happy. He remains disillusioned and feels as if something is missing. He lacks inner peace. He has, however, worked towards overcoming it – he has tried meditation, yoga, pranic healing, and other regimen as suggested by friends, colleagues, and family members – but to no use. He is becoming irritable day-by-day and complains about petty things like the geyser is not working properly, the electricity back up is not starting, the car is not clean, the food is spicy, the yoga teacher is late, the mobile signal is weak, the kids or the house staff are loud, and so on.

Misha always tries to pacify him and does everything possible to comfort her husband, but she too is stressed. To get a good night's sleep Sachin is now addicted to sleeping pills. As if by routine, Misha keeps all the needful on his bedside table each night exactly at 10.30 so that Sachin can sleep peacefully. She waits in the other room, watching TV, for him to sleep. Only then does she get up and go back to her room to sleep. She does not share any of her problems with Sachin fearing it will add to his worries.

Sachin often watches his house staff having meals and sharing their troubles with each other openly and light-heartedly. Whenever Sachin sees them laughing, he thinks how they can be happy despite so many problems in their lives. But he is not interested in them apart from the work they did and the salary he paid them.

He just wants to be happy from within, to sleep peacefully without the pill. He wants to be content with himself and seeks inner peace.

After trying almost everything, someone suggests that he join a month-long course on 'How to Be a Happy and Content Person' conducted by a baba, famously known as Smiling Baba, once a year in a luxury resort. Three weeks pass by while doing the course, but he is still not happy. He still faces problems back home and at work which makes him restless and irritable.

One day in that resort, he comes across his college friend, Mahendra, who seems to be a happy man, full of life. Sachin asks him if he too is following the course. Mahendra replies that he owns an advertising agency and has a two-year contract with the baba's company and has come here to renew the contract. Since this baba's business is booming, he wants to double the fee this time and hence has come personally for renewing the contract. He adds that he believes these courses are fake. But Sachin asks if he cannot see the 'divine smile' on baba's face while preaching. Mahendra scoffs and says he smiles when he sees so many high-class fools who have come to listen to his bullshit.

Sachin then discusses with Mahendra how he has tried all methods of attaining peace but has failed. He asks his friend how he carries that look of content and smile on his face.

Mahendra gives him a simple solution. He asks him to start watching the daily activities of his house and office staff and their conversations, because it is not luxury or material things that make us happy, but the simple sharing and caring for others' problems.

Sachin follows his advice and keenly watches them and listens to all their conversations for about ten days: the sweeper woman, almost forty years, is a victim of domestic violence, and the gardener is unable to send his son to school due to a lack of funds. They are all performing their duties despite major problems like fever and illness, leaking roofs, power cuts throughout the night, with a smile on their faces and living life with full zeal. He realizes that the poor do not complain much despite their miserable lives, whereas the rich are always cribbing even though they have everything simply because they do not share or care.

Sachin gives his gardener money to help with his son's education. He sends the sweeper woman's husband to a rehab centre for treatment. He helps all his staff as much as he can. He can now see them happier and praise him in their conversations. He feels as if he has not helped, but shared their grievances.

Within days he can feel a ray of contentment flowing inside him. Today, at night when Misha comes to her room after watching television, she is surprised to see the sleeping pill, eye mask, and water untouched by her husband's bedside.

Sachin is sleeping peacefully with a smile on his face.

Questions

How much wealth does it take to be happy and content?

What do we look for when we choose our ambitions in life?

32

PAGLI – THE CRAZY GIRL

A mentally challenged woman escapes from the Amritsar mental asylum and commits suicide on the railway tracks.

Even though the end is tragic, the story begins differently.

This story is about a girl named Pari, a sixteen-year-old girl studying in Class 10. She was the only daughter of a middle-class family. Her father had named her Pari, meaning 'an angel', his angel. Being the only child, she enjoyed the undivided love of both her parents. Her life was full of happiness until one day when both her parents died in a road accident while returning from a pilgrimage to Vaishno Devi. The loss was unbearable for Pari. She was shocked to the core, so much so that she could not utter a word.

Before leaving for the pilgrimage, her parents had sent Pari to stay with her Mama (maternal uncle). Following their death, it was decided that she would continue staying with him, as he was the only relative in the city and very close to the family. Pari had turned silent and would not show any emotion. She would sob when she saw her Mama's affection towards his children. She felt lonely and gradually lost all her confidence. Two months passed, but her grief kept increasing. One day when she was alone in the house, her Mama took advantage and sexually assaulted her. Due to her mental state, she could not raise a voice. Her Mama also threatened to throw her out of his house. She had nowhere else to go and because he was looking after all her expenses she thought it was her duty to obey him. He continued to assault her for four years, until she turned twenty. It was now time to get her married. In greed, Mama married her off to one of his clients, an old widower, who had a married daughter of almost Pari's age. This old man had seen Pari when he had visited their house and was attracted to her. He offered him a big amount of money. Finding it an opportunity to recover his past expenses on the girl, he agreed to the offer.

By now Pari's mental condition had deteriorated further. There was no resistance or refusal from her side. Maybe she had wanted to end the exploitation at her Mama's hands thinking one day her future will be secure. She hoped for a house and a husband of her own, even though it may not be of her choice or suitability.

Her marriage led her to yet another traumatic phase. The old man took a new drug to counter his impotency and forced himself on her every day. Pari, though still silent, was now entering a deeper phase of depression. She started doing abnormal activities in her daily life. After a while the medicines stopped having an effect on her husband which hurt his male ego. In frustration, one day he consumed four tablets and tried his vigour on her. But during the intercourse his heartbeat increased and he died on the spot, on top of Pari. This was the worst shock for Pari – a dead body on her in such a condition. It was the first and last time since her parents' death that she shouted and howled and cried. This trauma took a toll on her mind. Her stepdaughter threw her in a mental asylum and took over her father's house, leaving Pari homeless once again.

Life in the asylum was cruel to Pari. The sweeper sexually assaulted her whenever he got a chance. Frustrated by the daily torture, one day Pari fled from the asylum and reached the nearby railway station. She hurriedly boarded a train and managed to reach the last station, Amritsar. She kept sitting even after all passengers got off. The train was then taken to another track for cleaning and maintenance.

Here, a man in his late fifties, Malkit Singh, of the maintenance department of the railways, got on the train to check as per his duty. Hearing footsteps, Pari hid under the seat she was sitting on. Malkit Singh saw the feet of a girl and asked her to come out. She did not respond. Malkit Singh, seeing her condition and appearance, understood that she was not sane. He called his senior, the yard in-charge, who told him to call his wife for help. He brought his wife over and asked her to convince her to come out and go with them to their house. His wife did the needful and pampering her like a child persuaded her to go with them.

The first thing they did was to feed Pari. Malkit Singh's wife then cut her dishevelled hair short and gave her a bath and dressed her in fresh clothes of her own. This new look suited Pari well. She seemed like a totally changed person.

Malkit Singh's senior told them that they could not keep the girl there any longer. Malkit Singh and his wife, a childless couple, tried to convince him telling they will keep her at their home and take care of her as their daughter. But being illegal, he did not approve. He called for the railway police.

An inspector and two constables came to take Pari away. But Malkit Singh saw the inspector's lusting eyes, and fearing for her safety, asked him to sign a confirmation letter of custody of the girl. The inspector made a report, signed by two witnesses, and handed it over to the yard in-charge.

Unwillingly, Malkit Singh handed Pari over to the inspector who took her away in their police van to the government mental asylum. En route, the inspector ordered the driver to direct the van towards a secluded place. He told the constables to get down and started molesting Pari. One of the constables, a kind and sensitive man, tried to stop him, but his senior threatened to fire him. Helpless, he stood outside while the ruthless inspector sexually assaulted Pari inside the van. After the assault, they proceeded for the asylum. He handed her over to the head psychiatrist. The inspector hinted the doctor that though she was not mentally stable, she was cooperative in the presence of a handsome man. This gave the doctor a clear indication that the inspector had assaulted her. The same lust appeared in his eyes.

Three months have passed.

A crowd has gathered and they are talking about some woman who had committed suicide on the railway tracks near Malkit Singh's house. Malkit Singh also goes to check and is shocked to see Pari's body cut into two halves: a train had passed over her. He cries loudly and screams at his senior, also present there, who had ordered him to send Pari away to the butchers. Hearing this, the senior's eyes tear up out of guilt. Pari's assaulted lower body lies freed from her retarded mind.

Questions

Have we ever tried to rescue those who are not like us, exploited while roaming openly on the streets?

Do you think such people are safe in asylums?

ORPHANAGE

33

A REASON TO LIVE

Dhruv Mishra, a twenty-seven-year-old bachelor, teaches computer science to young children in an orphanage called Nanhi Jyoti (Little Flame). He is a well-settled IT engineer who works six days of the week in an MNC and teaches the kids here from 8 a.m. to 2 p.m. every Sunday.

It is a fine Sunday morning and the class is being held in the open grounds of the premises. Being early December, it is somewhat chilly, and everyone is enjoying the sun. Nanhi Jyoti is run by an NGO where many volunteer to teach the kids various subjects other than the usual course over weekends. Dhruv is one such volunteer, who has been coming here for the last two years. After his class, he spends an extra hour with the kids. He has lunch with them and talks to them. He looks forward to Sunday throughout the week. He spends the first half at the orphanage and evenings with friends over a session of poetry. Dhruv writes excellent poetry, and all his friends appreciate it. Sundays leave

Dhruv satisfied and rejuvenated, and help him go through the work week.

One Sunday, while taking his class in Nanhi Jyoti, Dhruv sees a young woman enter through the gates of the orphanage. She is visibly sad and anxious. She approaches him and asks for directions to the head warden's office. She is avoiding eye contact and is in a haste. Dhruv asks if she has joined the orphanage as a new staff or has come to make a donation. She has come to teach children drawing and painting, she answers. Dhruv asks her name. She just says, 'Drishti.' Without asking any further questions, Dhruv starts to introduce himself, but she still does not show interest.

Seeing she is not interested, Dhruv asks her, '*Tumhein bhi Mehta Sahab ne bheja hoga.*' (Did Mr Mehta send you here?)

Drishti is surprised as to how he knows.

Dhruv says with a smile, 'Welcome to the world of happiness!'

Curious, Drishti asks how he got here. Dhruv begins his story.

Dhruv stands at the window of his high-rise apartment, ready to jump off. He is shattered and disappointed and wants to end this useless life. He feels numb, but a bright hoarding suddenly catches his eye. It flashes, alternatively, *Give So That Others Can Live* and *Donate Your Organs.* There is a mobile number and an address mentioned underneath. This gets Dhruv thinking and he stays awake the whole night. He thinks he must make at least his death worthwhile and decides to donate his organs.

Next morning, he goes to the address mentioned on the hoarding, but there is nobody present at the desk. He sees a lot of empty forms lying on the desk. He picks up a form and starts filling it without wasting any time. As he is about to finish, the supervisor, also the head and in-charge of the centre, reaches his desk. He is a well-dressed man, with a name tag, *Dr Mehta*. Dhruv desperately asks him to take all his organs, whatever is usable and can help another person. Dr Mehta, also a psychiatrist, can read the signs of depression. He asks Dhruv into his office. To calm him down, he starts by asking about him: his name, age, profession, about his parents, family, financial condition, and so on. Dhruv feels comfortable and answers his questions that he is twenty-five, has a good job in an IT company that has provided him with a two-BHK flat, and that he got a promotion last month. He has loving parents, both retired teachers, who live in Dehradun, a younger brother who is studying and working in the US, and a sister, married and expecting her first child due next month. But when Dr Mehta asks about his marital status, Dhruv gets hyper and shouts, 'This is my personal matter. I won't answer your question, but I am not married.'

Dr Mehta now understands why Dhruv is suicidal. He says, '*Shaadi ke baare mein baat nahin karte, lekin tumhari koi girlfriend toh hogi?*' (Let's not talk about marriage, but you must have a girlfriend?)

On hearing this Dhruv immediately gets up and starts walking out of the office.

As he opens the door to leave, he hears Dr Mehta saying, '*Apne maa baap ke baare mein nahin socha. Apni chhoti behan, jo agle mahine Ma banne wali hai aur tum Mama. Apne chhote bhai ke baare mein bhi nahin, ke tumhare aise chale jaane se uspe kya asar padega? Bas ek ladki ke peechhe in sab ko chhodke chale ho?*' (You didn't spare your parents a thought. Nor your sister, who is going to be a mother next month, and you a Mama. Nor your younger brother, how will he survive without you? You are concerned only about one girl and are willing to leave everything for her?)

Dhruv is shocked to hear this and asks Dr Mehta how he knows that his girlfriend dumped him and that he is going to commit suicide.

Dr Mehta asks him to take his seat politely and makes him sit again. He is sixty-five, a retired psychiatrist from a government hospital, volunteers for this job, and has seen the world very closely through his many experiences. He says he understood his mental condition on reading his form. He explains that there are so many people in the world, especially children, who are not privileged like them, but still find happiness in small things. One can seek happiness in their joy. And as for marriage or finding true love, love will find you. Until then, he says, you should give your unconditional love to the needy, to those who are depressed and anxious, searching for their love to settle in life.

Back at the orphanage, Drishti, who was earlier avoiding eye contact, now looks into Dhruv's eyes and smiles. Dhruv gets up and says, '*Head warden se milwata hoon. Chalein?*' (Let me introduce you to the head warden. Shall we?)

Drishti seems happy. She takes a deep breath, looks up towards the sun, and breathes life into her soul. '*Chalo*' (Let's go), she says with a smile.

They talk and are walking very closely as they head towards the head warden's office.

Questions

Do we attach enough importance to what we have in our lives? Can small things give us happiness and meaning in our life?

Is love of only one kind, the romantic one or should we be equally aware of other kinds of love which comes with responsibility towards others?

34

A BIRTH ON THE ROAD

Laxmi, a nineteen-year-old girl living in the slums, is pregnant with her first child. She lives in a joint family with her husband, Ramesh, her mother-in-law, father-in-law, and younger brother-in-law and his wife who is almost her age. Because the family is poor, they cannot afford to go to a government hospital and have thus arranged for a delivery at home with the help of a midwife.

Laxmi's labour pain starts on Saturday around 2 a.m. She tolerates it until 8 a.m. and then the midwife is called for. She tries for some time, but is not able to deliver the baby. After waiting for another couple of hours and looking at Laxmi's worsening condition, she suggests the family take her to the nearby government hospital.

The family panics now. They neither have the money nor any conveyance to take Laxmi to the hospital. They cannot even call for an ambulance. They collect all the money they have at home, and even borrow from their neighbours, and call for a three-wheeler to take Laxmi to the hospital. But the rickshaw cannot enter the narrow slum roads. With great difficulty, Ramesh, his brother, and his mother carry Laxmi till where the rickshaw is parked. Since all four cannot fit in, Ramesh's brother tells them he will follow them on foot.

Laxmi is in terrible pain by now. She is sweating profusely and her hands and feet are ice cold. The driver is driving with great care. Just as they are about to reach the hospital, the vehicle halts. A large crowd has gathered opposite the hospital and the police has barricaded the road from both sides. Nobody is allowed to be on the road, not even by foot. They find out that the chief minister is expected to pass by this road in half an hour to attend a function nearby. The driver requests the policemen to make an exception and allow his rickshaw to pass, but no one is ready to risk their job for a poor person. Ramesh too requests the policemen, but they turn a deaf ear to his pleas. Ramesh gets agitated and starts shouting, but his brother controls him and tells him not to annoy the officers.

The driver, thinking of wining hearts by sympathy, suggests Ramesh to take Laxmi by foot across the road. Ramesh and his brother support Laxmi by both arms and try to cross the road, but they are stopped. No one, except two people, come forward to help them. The rest all watch as mere spectators. They try to cross the road forcibly, but the policemen start to beat their legs with their lathis.

Just then Laxmi's water bursts and she cannot even stand now. She is laid on one side of the road. Helpless, her mother-in-law sits beside her with one hand on Laxmi's forehead and the other on hers. Laxmi almost loses consciousness when a fleet of cars, the chief minister's cavalcade, is seen approaching the road. Around ten cars in front, then an ambulance, then two cars, then the CM's car, followed by a fire brigade and a procession of another ten cars. DSP Vijay Kumar and his constable Mohan Lal, who is driving, are in the car just ahead of the ambulance. Vijay Kumar spots a woman on the road side in miserable condition. He immediately orders Mohan Lal to stop the car so that the ambulance behind them can help her, but he is reluctant fearing the loss of his job. Sensing this, Vijay Kumar points his revolver at his face and Mohan Lal then stops the car. Vijay Kumar gets off the car and gestures the ambulance driver to open the ambulance doors. Ramesh, seeing the DSP calling him, understands and quickly carries Laxmi into the ambulance. On Vijay Kumar's orders the nurses inside start with the procedures.

The interruption of his journey irks the CM. His secretary gathers information and tells him of the happenings. Meanwhile, Vijay Kumar writes an email to the IG of police, stating that while as in-charge of the CM's cavalcade he will take the CM safely to his destination, he also needs to fulfill his humanitarian duty of saving the pregnant woman's life. He also writes that he is stepping down from his position before any action is taken on him, as he believes to leave his job gracefully just as he performed his duties.

The IG was unavailable at the moment, and in his absence, his daughter, a senior journalist, attends to her father's email. She is impressed by this officer's courage, and, without her father's knowledge, breaks the news to her associated channels.

Still having to wait, the CM calls up the IG and orders him to fire Vijay Kumar, but he is still unavailable. Just then his secretary shows him the breaking news of the courageous act of Vijay Kumar and his resignation.

After a while, the IG returns the call to the CM and apologizes for not attending to it as he was performing a puja. But the CM is now aware of Vijay Kumar's status following the news, and realizes that firing Vijay Kumar would mean risking his position and reputation. So he cunningly changes his stance and orders him to promote Vijay Kumar as the new SP, praising that he had fearlessly fulfilled his duty towards humanity. He adds that the IG must mention that the CM has personally recommended the officer's promotion.

The CM gulps back his anger. His secretary, who has been watching all this silently, smiles mischievously, and says, '*Isiliye to janaab itne saalon se is post pe hain, kyunki waqt ke chaal ke saath badalna to koi aapse seekhe*' (It is for this reason I have stuck to my post for so many years; one has to learn how to change with the changing times from you.)

Questions

Do we need to keep aside our humanitarian responsibilities to carry out our job?

Is it worth taking on authority and power to be human and help the needy?

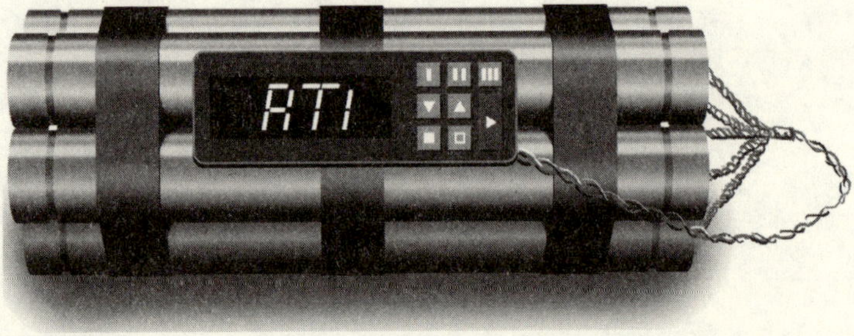
RTI

35

RIGHT TO INFORMATION

The Right to Information Act, simply known as RTI, is a revolutionary Act that aims to promote transparency in government institutions in India. The Act came into existence in 2005, after sustained efforts of anti-corruption activists.

It is termed revolutionary because it opens government organizations up for scrutiny. Equipped with knowledge about RTI, a common man can demand any government agency to furnish information. The organization is bound to provide the information, that too within 30 days, failing which the officer concerned is slapped with a monetary fine.

The basic objective of the Right to Information Act is to empower the citizens, promote transparency and accountability in the working of the Government, reduce corruption, and make our democracy work for the people in real sense.

Neelesh Sachdev is an RTI activist and a social reformer. He is a dedicated and honest person who tries to do his bit for the society by exposing corruption, and also helping the dishonest ones reform themselves into good citizens. He believes the aim is not only to expose their negatives, but to also help them take a positive turn. So far he has exposed many IPS, IAS, IFS, and other high officials, and thus has made many enemies. But at the same time he is brave and remains undeterred under any circumstances.

These days Neelesh has been working on a Naxalite group in Patna and is trying to convince its leader to surrender to the police assuring that he will help him get minimal punishment and provide rehabilitation to their group. For the latter he plans to seek his uncle's help. His uncle Satish Sachdev is the IG of police in Patna.

On the occasion of his birthday, Satish hosts a dinner party at his house and invites his close friends and relatives. Neelesh seeks this as a good opportunity to discuss the matter with him. When he arrives at his uncle's house, he is surprised to see some very famous but corrupt politicians and high officials, including two he had exposed in the past. Enmity is visible in their eyes. Neelesh is in a dilemma to see the kind of friendship they share with his uncle, whom he has always considered an honest and dedicated man.

The next morning he visits his uncle at his office. Satish assures his nephew that he will put in a special recommendation for minimum punishment to the Naxalite leader. With this assurance, Neelesh convinces the Naxalite to surrender. After a week, Neelesh goes to Satish's office for some work. He overhears him talking with the two corrupt officers he saw at his uncle's party and is shocked to learn that he is involved with them and other politicians in different conspiracies. He is about to escape unseen when Satish notices him and calls for him. Unable to control his disappointment, Neelesh lashes out at his uncle threatening to expose him. Satish is now afraid and tries to delude Neelesh, but his nephew storms out threatening to file an RTI against him.

Satish can by no means afford defamation, so he plans a conspiracy against his nephew along with some of his junior officers. He hides a big amount of money and drugs in Neelesh's house and gets a raid conducted. The recovery of these goods leads to Neelesh's arrest. He even frames him for having connections with the Naxalites and portrays him as a terrorist. The Naxalite leader, whom Neelesh had convinced to surrender, is pressurized to give a statement regarding Neelesh's involvement in supplying them with arms and ammunition. Neelesh is withheld under a remand of five days and then to be presented in court. On Satish's orders, he is beaten and tortured physically as well as mentally. But Neelesh remains undeterred and does not cave in to their demands of confessing to be a terrorist.

The police officers are now in a fix – Neelesh has not confessed and he is in no physical condition to be produced in court. Under the guidance of Satish, they plan to kill him off in a fake encounter on their way to the court. But the thorn in their plan comes in the form of an honest police constable, Rajnath, who will accompany them to the court. On the day of the trial, Neelesh is carried to the court in a police van. They drive through a secluded road where they first kill Rajnath with his own gun and then a senior officer shoots Neelesh. The story that is portrayed to the media and court is as follows: on way to the court, there is a scuffle wherein Neelesh snatches Rajnath's gun, kills him, and tries to escape, but the senior officer stops him by shooting at him, thereby killing Neelesh.

With this, Neelesh becomes a proven criminal working for the anti-social elements in the country. In the guise of an RTI activist, he had been filing such applications to malign the reputation of senior officials because of his connections with the enemy countries who wanted to defame Indian politicians.

Breaking News

A terrorist named Neelesh is killed.

IG Satish is honoured for unearthing the conspiracy of an enemy country and also for eliminating a terrorist.

Naxalite leader is spared with minimum punishment as the police weakens the case against him.

Constable Rajnath receives a bravery award posthumously for bravely fighting against a terrorist.

Neelesh's family – his mother, wife, and twelve-year-old son – are boycotted from society, and flee the country, away from the insults and taunts.

Facts

With more than sixty-five people killed and close to four hundred harassed or intimidated, violence against RTI activists is a menace that continues even today.

Questions

Have the murderers of RTI activists who have been killed till date been imprisoned or brought to justice?

Have the RTI activists turned silent and gone into hiding because of the threats to their lives and their families?

36

SHOR – THE NOISE

Bhumi, a twenty-one-year-old girl, lives with her mother and younger brother in the congested streets of Chandni Chowk in Delhi. Her mother has been diagnosed with third-stage cancer. Her brother, Ashish, is not smart, but is very hard-working. Despite practicing, he got a compartment in his Class 12 boards in mathematics. It has been two years since their father went to Dubai to work. Their financial condition is not very sound, but they are living with whatever money their father sends.

Life in this house is tough. They live on the second floor without any proper ventilation, and air-conditioners or coolers are luxuries unheard of. There are often fights among the neighbours, thereby creating a menace on the streets. Social functions keep taking place inside the already congested colony, causing a lot of dirt, traffic jams, and noise.

Bhumi's mother was diagnosed with cancer around three months back. Her father had come during her diagnosis, but had to leave in a week's time, else he would have been fired. He gave Bhumi some money for the treatment and has been sending more in small instalments from Dubai. Her mother is quite fragile having undergone four sessions of chemotherapy. She faces severe side effects like body pains, especially during the first two days, loss of appetite, hair loss, and bad skin. Running the house and caring for her mother with limited means is very difficult, but Bhumi has been managing.

One Sunday while taking her mother for her fifth chemotherapy session, they see huge tents, music systems, and idols on tempos approaching their street – signs of a *jagrata* (gathering). Today her mother has developed a new side effect. She has a rash all over her body by the time they reach home in the evening. Being a Sunday, no doctor is available. So, Bhumi gets the medicines prescribed over the phone and gives them to her mother. But there is no relief; the rash worsens. Bhumi also has to help her brother with maths for his examination the following day. He is panicking. This is his only chance to get admitted to a college.

To make matters worse, the jagrata begins. The noise neither lets her mother sleep nor allows her brother to study. Bhumi puts earplugs in her mother's ears to lessen the noise, but as she is already in great discomfort due to the rash, she finally pulls them out and throws them aside. Bhumi calls the doctor who now suggests an intravenous injection to be given. She rushes to the chemist and tells Ashish to try and study on his own. She fetches a person to administer the injection.

It is almost 11 p.m. and nobody has eaten anything. Bhumi makes parathas for Ashish and herself and some khichri for her mother and feeds her. By this time, her mother's allergy has reduced and though she is feeling better she is still unable to sleep because of the noise. Even Ashish is getting worried as he is not able to study properly. Bhumi goes downstairs and requests the hosts to lower the volume, but they all turn a deaf ear. They advise her to not interfere with the bhakti or else the goddess will punish her. Ashish now tells his sister to make a police complaint to stop the music. Although reluctant initially, she then calls up the police station. But the constable tells her he is alone at the police station and everyone else had gone to the same jagrata for security measures. He tells her that the organizers of the jagrata are very influential people and that she should not interfere or disturb them. Hearing this Ashish gets angry and wants to go downstairs to fight, but Bhumi calms him.

Bhumi now turns to Roshan Lal, one of the organizers and an acquaintance, for help. But he tells her it is just a matter of two hours and that they should cooperate. Bhumi sees the owner of the chemist watching the jagrata. She pleads with the owner to give her mother a sedation injection. But the shop has already closed and he refuses. Bhumi is near tears. Seeing her condition, the pharmacy owner suggests a painkiller patch for Bhumi's mother, a new invention which could be applied easily on the back for instant pain relief and help get sleep. Though it was expensive, Bhumi buys it and applies it on her mother's back, and she gets relief from pain.

It is around 2.30 a.m. now. Both Bhumi and Ashish are waiting for the jagrata to get over in half an hour. The clock strikes 3. But suddenly they hear the crowd demanding another two to three *bhenta*s (songs). Bhumi and Ashish have no other option but to wait again. The jagrata finally gets over around 4.30 a.m.

Bhumi and Ashish breathe a sigh of relief. Bhumi gets up to open the windows to let some fresh air in. Ashish asks Bhumi to clarify some three or four difficult maths problems. She starts helping out her brother when again sound erupts over the loudspeaker at 5.11 am. This time, it is the azaan from the nearby mosque.

Helplessly, both the siblings look at each other.

Questions

Should religious functions be allowed to undermine our rights as citizens?

Is it possible for functionaries to keep aside their religious beliefs when enforcing law and order?

37

BROTHER

Yogesh is a thirty-three-year-old businessman living in a penthouse apartment in a posh locality in Delhi with his wife, Vidya, an eight-year-old daughter, Ayesha, and a five-year-old son, Shivam. But he is also a pervert. Vidya trusts her husband and is unaware of his roving eye, unlike their maid, Malini. Well aware of his intentions, Malini is very conscious while doing her chores in the house.

Ayesha is very good in painting and has won a prize at school. While she has asked her parents for a big set of painting materials as reward, Shivam wants a new cricket set. Vidya has promised them these if they perform well in their examinations.

It is the day of the parent–teacher meeting at school. The teachers want to speak to the parents about their children's performance the past year and also to provide books and stationery for the next session. Vidya asks Yogesh to accompany her to the school and on their way back buy the promised gifts for their children. But Yogesh has not been keeping well and excuses himself from attending the meeting. He instructs Balwant, their elderly and sincere driver, to keep an eye on his wife and children while they go to the crowded market. He always suspects eve-teasers.

As Vidya is about to leave for school, Malini urges to leave as she has almost finished her day's work; just the floor needs to be mopped, which she will do the next day. She is afraid of being in the house alone with Yogesh. But Vidya tells her to finish her chores because she is expecting her in-laws later in the day.

Malini is very uncomfortable and goes about her chores hurriedly. But she notices Yogesh staring at her from his room. She covers herself up carefully, finishes her work, and leaves in a haste, asking Yogesh to lock the door.

Yogesh is all alone at home. While he is shaving, the doorbell rings. In the CCTV camera installed in the lobby, he can see a young sales girl at the door with a big bag on her shoulders. He hurriedly finishes up, combs his hair, opens the door, and asks the purpose of her visit. She is here to promote a new range of stationery and sports equipment for children, the company she is working for has launched, at a ten percent discount.

But Yogesh has lust in his mind. He shows interest and invites her inside to show all products. He casually sits next to her on the same two-seater sofa and initiates a conversation. After some hesitation, she too becomes comfortable thinking him to be a decent man and starts discussing her personal life – she is unmarried and lives in Subhash Nagar.

He selects a lot more than needed – painting material for Ayesha, and even places order for a cricket set, which would be delivered via courier in a couple of days, and some other toys for Shivam. Seeing him buy so much, she becomes even more casual with him.

Yogesh goes to the kitchen to get her some refreshments. He also calls up Vidya and asks her to not buy the gifts for the kids, instead tells her to take them out for lunch, and disconnects the call immediately, not giving her a chance to question anything.

He now goes to her with the credit card to make the payment. But when he is about the punch the last digit of his PIN, the sales girl, unintentionally and happily, thanks him, 'My day's target has been met. I need not stray more for sales and can go home directly from here. Thank you, Bhaiya.'

Bhaiya? His ears hurt with the sound of that word, and he enters the wrong digit. The transaction is declined.

Disappointed, Yogesh cancels the order. The sales girl is confused and asks Yogesh what the matter is, but he is no longer interested in her. He bluntly says he is not interested in buying her products anymore.

The girl leaves the house without any sales.

Questions

Do we respect women enough in our society? Is Yogesh the odd one out or do men generally behave this way? Is there a problem with our social conditioning?

38

THE THEFT

Satish, a rich businessman, lives in a bungalow of almost 1,100 square yards, in a posh colony in Delhi with his wife, Reema, a housewife, who is distrustful and hence strict with her house staff. They have two children, an eighteen-year-old son and a twenty-one-year-old daughter. Reema trusts only Raju, their forty-two-year-old chef, that too not wholeheartedly, and his wife, Sita, is the next privileged one, the only one who is allowed in the house, but not more than two or three hours, to do the dusting. Even Raju is not allowed to enter the rooms apart from the kitchen without permission.

Satish and Reema's children are pampered to such an extent that they do not care to respect their staff, not even Raju and Sita who have been serving them relentlessly for the last twenty years.

Raju and Sita have an eighteen-year-old daughter who lives in the village with Raju's parents. She had been engaged when she was barely ten years and now the date for her marriage, due in three months, has been fixed. But both parents are worried because her future in-laws have demanded an unthinkable amount of a lakh as dowry. On top of that there will be additional expenses of the wedding. Raju requests Satish to loan him the amount, but Satish refuses and says he can give him only twenty thousand as advance. Although Reema is fond of gold jewellery, the children are spendthrift, and the house has an over-abundance of money; they are not willing to help out Raju in his hour of need.

Reema has got new gold necklace and earrings made for herself and is showing them to Satish at night in their bedroom when Raju knocks at the door and comes inside to give Satish his medicines, as he does every night. Reema immediately tries to hide the jewellery, but the necklace slips and falls from her hand. The kind Raju gently picks it up and gives it to her before leaving the room. Reema keeps the jewellery in her bedside drawer.

The following morning, as per routine, Reema goes for her walk at 8. When she returns, she remembers that she had kept the jewellery in her bedside drawer. When she goes to safely keep them in the almirah, she finds the necklace is missing. She panics and starts shouting. Satish asks what the matter is, and Reema, without sparing a second thought, accuses Raju of stealing her necklace.

Raju is laying out the table for breakfast when he hears Reema's accusations. She threatens to call the police if he does not confess. Raju defends himself saying that he has been a loyal servant all through the years he has served them. He begs them to not call the police because that will tarnish his reputation and may prove to be the reason for his daughter's wedding to be called off.

Sita has been watching the entire episode, alas, as a mere spectator. She tries to defend her husband. All the pleading falls on deaf ears. Raju is arrested and is taken into police custody. He is beaten up in order to confess his crime, the crime which he could never even have thought of committing.

The next day Sita goes to the jail to meet Raju. Seeing his condition, she breaks down and confesses that it was she who stole the necklace.

That night, when Raju returned the necklace to Reema, he had discussed it with his wife, saying he wished their master would lend him the money he had asked for. Sita had listened to it and got carried away, and the next morning, in the absence of the couple in the room, stole the necklace. She had thought they would never be suspected because they were the only trusted staff and an incident like theft had never occurred in the household. But Raju's condition jolts Sita. She confesses her crime to Satish and Reema, and begs them to release Raju.

Both Satish and Reema are shocked at first, and then furious. But after immense pleading, Sita succeeds in getting them to free Raju on the condition that both of them will not be paid for the next one year and will not be allowed to take any leaves in this duration. Sita does not have an option but to agree.

Satish does not want to keep the couple employed any longer, but Reema argues that Raju is a good cook and everyone is used to the taste of his food. Moreover, Raju is so responsible and dedicated that Reema does not have to worry about running the household. He is aware of everyone's likes and dislikes and manages everything smoothly.

The next day Raju is brought home. He is so angry with Sita that he is not ready to even talk to her. He feels guilty as well as embarrassed. Because of this incident, both Satish and Reema, every now and then, lecture the two on ethics, morality, and honesty to keep their guilt alive and to make a point of how generous they are towards them.

Meanwhile, a servant, also working in Reema's friend's house, belonging to the same village as Raju, shares this incident back home. Overnight, Raju's status is shattered and his daughter's wedding is called off. Raju's parents believe it is a direct consequence of their actions. Raju's mother is not able to bear the shock and soon dies, and his father, already too old, cannot not guarantee his granddaughter's security anymore.

Raju does not know how to ask his master to allow his daughter to stay with them in their house. One day he gathers courage and asks for their permission. He adds that she will work and they do not need to pay her. Reema likes the idea and they fire the car cleaner and outhouse cleaner so that Raju's daughter can be given that job. Raju, Sita, and their daughter are thankful for the courteous gesture of their masters, and work tirelessly like slaves without any salary. They feel even more guilty of betraying such good, generous masters.

Three months pass and things are getting back to normal.

One day, while the masters are away on a vacation to London, the same inspector who had arrested Raju, along with three other policemen and three well-dressed men, arrive at the house. Raju is afraid that they are here to arrest him again. He hesitates to open the door because his master is not present to protect him. When the inspector threatens to break the door, Raju opens it slowly and immediately falls at the inspector's feet and begs him to not arrest him.

But the inspector is not here to arrest him, but Satish and Reema. Together they have committed a fraud of twelve hundred crores and have transferred great amounts to foreign banks. He also tells him that Raju was arrested without an FIR only because of Satish's pressure and connections with top police officials. No case was registered against him.

Raju is shocked to hear about the amount of fraud. He tells the inspector of Satish and Reema's whereabouts in London. The police is helpless and return empty-handed.

After the police leave, Raju wonders who the bigger criminal is.

Questions

Is it justified that the bigger criminals escape trial while the smaller ones get caught in the net?

Do people commit a crime always with malicious intent or is there a distinction between criminals who have to fight for their survival and those who are already privileged?

भारतीय
₹500

39
IMPOTENT

A popular Babaji (Godman) is making an appeal on national television:

I am Shivpujan Singh, just another ordinary farmer's son from a small village in western Uttar Pradesh. My father was a hardworking farmer, who had a small piece of land from where he fed his family – an ailing mother, a helpful wife, three daughters, and two sons.

I am the youngest and the most pampered one in the family.

My sick grandmother was very religious, she never missed her prayers, even when she was unwell. She prayed four times a day. She adored me and always blessed me with good health.

From giving birth to four children before me and because of poverty, my mother was physically weak; which led to my premature birth, in the seventh month of her pregnancy. Although she was mentally a strong woman, who stood by my father through many adversities, the responsibilities of the household took a toll on her health.

My mother was a noble woman, an example of sacrifice. She rarely ever ate her fill, always paying more attention to everyone else. My father too took good care of everyone and attended to everyone's needs. Despite limited means, he financially supported his married sister whose husband was an alcoholic and would beat her. My father's income came from his agricultural land of two acres. But the drought during my mother's last pregnancy changed the economics of our small house. So my mother sacrificed more during those turbulent times, neglecting herself while I grew inside her.

One unfortunate day, while she was doing her daily chores, she had to be rushed to the nearby village clinic where I was born two months before the due date. I was kept by the clinic under special care for more than two weeks, without taking any fee from my parents. I was too weak and there was faint hope of my survival, but the doctor did not spare any effort to save me. The result is in front of you, telling my story at the age of seventy-two.

After my delivery, my mother never recovered and remained undernourished till I last saw her. My grandmother died when I was six. My father's sister died at thirty-seven, when one day her alcoholic husband hit her on her head with a steel rod. My three elder sisters got married before they turned eighteen, as is the norm in our society. My elder brother started helping my father in the fields, relieving him of his responsibilities.

Now the focus was on me.

Most of the boys in our own and nearby villages were illiterate. But my parents as well as my brother wanted me to become an educated person and bring respect to the family.

I had, and still have, a weak, narrow, underweight body, but a sharp mind. I studied in a village government school till Class 10. There were only three teachers in the school including the principal. The class composition was thirty-odd boys and five or six girls. The few progressive-minded parents sent their girls to the school, but only two of them could make it to the tenth standard. Though our village was the biggest in our district and had a village panchayat, the mentality of the elders was backward: they did not want the girls of the village to attend school with boys. Since there was no other all-girls school, most of them were forced to drop out or were married off.

I was in Class 9 when I was engaged to a girl called Lakshmi. She was in Class 6 and a very bright student. Our school principal had once announced that Lakshmi will make her parents and the entire village proud one day after completing her higher education. But this wish could not be fulfilled because her parents removed her from the school after her engagement with me.

Lakshmi held me responsible for her shattered dreams; she wanted to become a graduate one day. But she could not raise her voice against the village sarpanch and the other elders because our society does not allow the boy and the girl to see each other during the courtship period.

In Class 10, I got influenced by the son of the sarpanch, Ajit, two years elder to me, and a drug addict. He even visited sex workers. He became my best friend and we went to the town together to watch adult movies near the red light area, where drugs were also available. I started smoking up and soon became an addict. I became attracted to women who were available for only a few rupees in the dingy, stinking streets of the old city of Meerut.

I failed my first attempt to make physical contact with a sex worker. I could not perform because of my weak physique and also because I had smoked up before going to her. She questioned my manhood, and her taunts haunt me till today. The failure led me into depression and I fell heavily into drugs. The next time I went to a brothel with Ajit, I tried, but failed again. The woman helped me overcome my anxiety. But I failed yet again.

This woman asked me to spend the next night with her so she could give me lessons on lovemaking. She was also trying to act smart and secure me as a permanent client. I was too embarrassed to even look into her eyes and left the dingy cabin, where a bench was laid to perform the act. When asked, I lied to Ajit saying I had a good time. I was ashamed to be labelled 'impotent' in my friends' circle.

The grief and tension of my sexual inadequacy resulted in depression. I began to lose self-confidence. It was not soon after my father came to know about my drug addiction. My mother was worried about my declining health. To bring me out of this, without consulting anyone my father got me married to Lakshmi soon after I passed the tenth standard. I had earned the title of an educated person, which brought back some of the lost confidence, but the first night with Lakshmi proved to be too heavy and too long for me.

Yet again I was unable to perform. Lakshmi was quite modern in her thinking. She believed in living a parallel life with her husband, even participate equally while making love. In spite of her best efforts, I failed again and again, but being a good Indian wife with good values, Lakshmi kept trying. I was taking drugs secretly to kill my depression, but this made me fall into acute depression. My parents and brother wanted me to come out of this addiction. Unlike the other men in the village, I did not take drugs for mere entertainment, but to escape the harsh reality.

Three years into my marriage, one day on my brother's orders I was to go to the city to buy pesticides. My sister-in-law had gone to her parents' house with the kids and my parents were away to the next village visiting an ailing relative. But I missed the bus because I was smoking up on way to the bus stop and had fallen asleep. So I returned home, thinking I would fulfil the duties the next day.

When I reached my house, the door to my room was locked from inside. I thought Lakshmi must be sleeping. But what I saw shocked me: Lakshmi and my elder brother in a compromising position! They both confronted me without any fear or shame. Lakshmi told me she went to my brother to satiate her physical needs when her husband could not fulfil them. My brother said it is good she went to him and not to someone else, which would have brought disgrace to the entire family. This way the family's honour remained within the family itself.

I could not bear this humiliating defeat at the hands of my wife and brother, and immediately left the house and took the last bus to the city, never to come back again. I spent a few days on the benches at the railway station, bus station, and public parks until one day I met my cousin from my village at the railway station who told me to go back home as Lakshmi was pregnant.

Of course he did not know the truth. To protect myself from further disgrace, I told him that I would go home the next day.

Before meeting my cousin, I was thinking of returning home because I could not live without the comforts, especially without my drugs, but hearing this news I felt it was better to commit suicide than return.

I went to the river bank, but before jumping in my eyes caught the figure of a holy man sitting outside his hut facing the river and performing his prayers. He was old with long hair and a beard, and wore long, loose orange clothes, a mark of the godmen in our country. He had a calm look on his face. I got pulled into his aura. I went up to him and bowed my head before his feet. He opened his eyes and looked at me carefully. Judging the state of my mind, he offered me food and shelter, and counselled me. From that day I became his disciple.

Soon, word spread that this holy man has healing powers, that he saved a dying man he found on the river bank, too weak and sick to survive. That man was me. More people started visiting him to seek his blessings and magical powers to heal the ailing. I slowly gained health and attained peace of mind while with him. But I continued smoking weed, and Babaji became my active partner in this addiction. I started dressing up like him. Very soon his modest hut was converted into an ashram. The number of followers kept increasing, as did the revenue. We could now afford to house over twenty permanent disciples on pay roll.

One day a billionaire businessman suffering from cancer came to Babaji to seek his blessings. This time Babaji performed a special puja for him for a fee. The sick man was getting treatment done from the US alongside. He recovered, but all credit was given to our Babaji. He donated thirty acres of land, millions in cash, and even a luxury car to him.

Looking at the overwhelming response, Babaji started building a *dera*.[1] But we did not have to spend a dime because the devotees took over the responsibility with their own money. This dera became a monument of luxury, a palace. Business flourished, Babaji did not live long enough to see its growth: he died a year after the inauguration of the dera. He died of a cardiac arrest. The businessman, his patron, too died due to a relapse of his cancer. This time no magical powers or medical treatment could save him.

Being the closest to Babaji, I was made in-charge of the ever-flourishing dera. We even started our own television channel, *Bhakti mein Shakti*. Our worth has increased and we crossed the 12,000 crores mark last year.

Oh, I forgot to tell you about my family I left behind in the village. My wife, my illegitimate son, and my brother's widow live in my palace now. They were living under miserable conditions after the death of my parents and brother. Here, they are no more than staff to me. I allowed them to stay here just to satisfy my own hurt ego.

Devotees think that I have the magical powers to cure sick bodies, that I have a direct connection with god. I do not wish to break their faith because it is due to this that I live like their god today. The best part of this business is that the one who does not recover, or dies, after seeking my blessings feels that it is god's will, and do not speak ill of me, but the ones whose wishes are fulfilled sing my praises.

My Baba Business keeps flourishing each day. WhatsApp, Facebook, Twitter, Instagram, TV channels, word of mouth, seminars, and public appearances have made me so powerful that most of the politicians, top businessmen, and government officials come to me to fulfil their selfish interests.

All this changed last month, when I, the Babaji, suffered a stroke – that too while performing a puja – that has left the right side of my body paralysed. The faith of my disciples in my magical powers made me pray for my health tirelessly, but my condition worsened without medical assistance. Millions of my followers thought it is because my body has taken a toll healing others. They prayed for me across my ashrams, which have now spread across the country and beyond, but nothing worked.

I finally gave up hope and insisted my staff to take me to the hospital, but my family that lives in my palace opposed this because they have been eyeing my wealth. Finally after much insistence, I was admitted to the hospital under the care of the most experienced team of physicians. In five weeks I recovered more than fifty per cent, and was sent back to my palace. Two nurses and a physiotherapist have been appointed here to take care of me. I hope to recover fully.

I wish that I had insisted on this kind of medical assistance earlier. I wish it were available when I was born premature and was weak all through my childhood, when I first started taking drugs, when I failed to satisfy Lakshmi, when I suffered from depression.

My bank accounts are filled with billions – rupees, dollars, pounds, dirhams. I have a big fleet of cars and even a private jet, but not a single ambulance. I have eighty-nine deras, ashrams, bhakti kendras, and meditation centres in India and abroad, but not a single hospital or a clinic. I have seven spiritual halls for meditation, but not even one for medication. My devotees have collected millions from the large-hearted followers to build another twelve-acre ashram in Ahmedabad.

I request all my followers to stop donating to us Babas. We cannot cure people. We do not possess any magical abilities. The only ability we have is to use god and religion to fool the innocent to accumulate wealth, name, and fame.

This addiction to name and fame is more dangerous than the addiction to smoking or drugs.

Today, I have made this public appearance to announce that I have decided to convert all my deras, centres, palaces, land, and everything else I own, into schools, hospitals, orphanages, skill-development centres, and old-age homes. I request my followers to keep donating like before, but from today it will be towards the benefit of the underprivileged children of god.

Keep trusting humanity.

Questions

Are Babas the rightful owner of the wealth they accumulate? How can humanity be served if Babas are made to give up their wealth?

40
MY SUNDAY FATHER

Mohit is a thirty-two-year-old marketing head of a company in Mumbai. He started his career at the age of twenty-five as a marketing professional and climbed the ladder of success swiftly with hard work and ambition. He is married to his college friend, Mayra, and they have a three-year-old daughter, Aahna, and they have a car and a house of their own.

He moved from his native town of Amritsar to the city that never sleeps. Like his city, Mohit's mind never sleeps. He dreams of becoming the branch head of the company – the present branch head will be retiring next year – and the CEO of the Indian division within the next five years. He wants to achieve all this before he turns forty.

His ambition has now made him so cunning that he does not think twice before working against his ethics and morality. He does not have time for his sick mother and his two sisters. The younger sister is unmarried, and his mother worries about her marriage. Mohit keeps telling her to wait until the next year when he hopes to become the branch head, and then he will bring his mother over to their company apartment and find a suitable groom for his sister. Until then he sends money back home regularly.

Mohit thinks he is taking good care of his family by fulfilling their worldly needs. But Mayra misses spending time with her husband and Aahna is too young to understand what it means to have a loving and caring father. Mayra pleads with her husband to cut down on business travel to spend time with the family, but Mohit's ambition does not allow him to break free from work.

Moreover, Mohit perceives a young employee, Sandeep, as a potential threat and has to spend more time at work to prove his worth in order to become the branch head. Just last week he failed to please his boss and to make up for this, he invites him for dinner at his house. Knowing his boss' flirtatious nature, he even requests Mayra to encourage and please him. Hearing this Mayra is shocked and loses any respect left for her husband.

Mayra is sticking it out with Mohit for the sake of their daughter. He knows the state of children when their parents separate. Mayra's sadness is noticed by Aahna's teacher, Vineet, who suggests her to join the school as a teacher which she agrees to. She joins Aahna's school as a painting teacher hoping to bring back colour to her life.

Vineet is the gymnastics teacher in the Kindergarten school and also the son of the owner of the school. He is a handsome unmarried man of 29 years who was a professional footballer and a football coach in a sports academy. He had separated from his girlfriend because she could not wait anymore to settle down in life because of her family's pressure but Vineet did not want to get married till he was playing for the National Football Team.

So, Vineet is now single and has started to take care of Mayra and her emotional needs. They have been in constant touch during school hours and after that over the phone. Their relation is nourished by his caring gestures and it soon grew further to a physical one. So now he takes care of both her missing needs, emotional and physical.

They have become lovers and spend a lot of time together after the school time in Mayra's home. Mayra had no guilt regarding her extra marital relations with Vineet because she lost her faith in Mohit when he had asked her to flirt with his boss. Though after a few days, when things calmed, Mohit thought that all was normal, but Mayra was no more the same old person.

In Vineet she finds a friend and also support. They become attached to each other to the extent Aahna starts calling him Papa because of the love he showers on her. Mohit is unaware of this new relationship because he is always tied up with work. It is only on Sundays he stays home and communicates little with his wife and daughter.

Finally the day arrives that Mohit has been waiting for one whole year. His flattery and hard work earns him the title of the new branch head. Dreams have turned into reality.

The first person he thinks of is his wife and reaches home early to share the news. But he is surprised to see a stranger answer the door. Vineet confidently introduces himself as his wife's friend and his daughter's teacher. Mayra is shocked to see her husband in the house at this hour. Aahna too is confused to see her father today because she sees him only on Sundays.

Mohit is angry and he understands what is going on. He now sees in Vineet a rival. To hide his emotions, he shares the news of his promotion with Mayra, but she expresses no happiness. She asks Aahna to congratulate her, but she asks innocently, 'Which Papa? Sunday wale Papa?' (My Sunday father?)

Questions

Do our ambitions at work take us away from our family and relationships to a point of no return?

Is it always a choice between professional growth or being with your family or is it a careful balance of these which should be the ideal of our modern lives?

41

WISH TO BE A DOG

Eight-year-old Lata, along with her friends, Mukesh and Radha, live in Bawana on the outskirts of Delhi. They are ragpickers. They collect plastics, papers, and other such items from morning till evening and then sell them for a meagre amount to buy food. These days they have to work very hard to find these items on the roads as the garbage collectors collect and throw garbage in the dumpyards.

Today, as any other day, the three start their work. Mukesh says, '*Yeh Swachh Bharat Abhiyan to humein bhookha hi maar dega*' (The Swachh Bharat Mission will make us go hungry.) Lata and Radha agree. They decide to go straight to the dump yard because the roads are mostly clean. When they reach, they find many stray dogs feeding in the dump. They are scared, but have no option, so they quietly begin sifting through the garbage when they suddenly hear the dogs bark. Even before they know, the dogs attack them.

Mukesh and Radha manage to escape with minor injuries and run straight to a police patrol van parked at a distance. They plead with the policemen to save their friend Lata, who will be eaten alive by the dogs if they do not help. But the policemen heartlessly reply, 'Don't you know the laws of our country? We cannot beat or kill dogs as it is punishable under the new laws.'

After a while, when the policemen see the children weep continuously, one of them agrees to go with them. On reaching the site, they find Lata's big polythene bag covered with blood, lying on the dusty ground. The dogs had dragged her to a distance and were eating her body.

Mukesh and Radha are inconsolable.

Radha questions the policeman, 'Isn't it better to be a dog than a poor child, in *this* country, where the law protects the dogs, not its children?'

Questions

Should the stray dogs be abandoned on the roads free to kill anybody?

Should the government not make animal shelter homes for the stray dogs?

ACKNOWLEDGEMENTS

I am a fifty something man with a nine-to-five work life, a big family with bigger responsibilities. As much as we would like to believe we are more than that, the sum of our parts, the inertia of our lives forces us to often feel otherwise. When I chose to escape that inertia through writing, I knew words won't be enough. This book holds not just words, but also courage, belief and hope. Not just mine, but of those around me.

My stories made me realize that writing requires more than just words. They cease to matter without a platform, for which I would like to thank Prasun, editorial director of Pan Macmillan India and also the editor of this book. He is the man who didn't just bear, but also corrected my rather loose grip on grammar and the *angrezi* language. I am grateful to Pan Macmillan India, for putting their ethics before their economics and publishing my short stories – something I feel is dying, but so important.

My wife Jasmina, has always supported me without questions or even reason. Thank you for understanding my passion and calling. I cannot forget to thank Gagandeep, my younger brother who allows me to manoeuver our otherwise taxing work hours, so that I can write. These people have given up something that they could've rather done for themselves, only to make sure that I am able to do something for myself.